ALSO BY PETER BOWEN

Badlands
Ash Child
Cruzatte and Maria
The Stick Game
Long Son
Thunder Horse
Notches
Wolf, No Wolf
Specimen Song
Coyote Wind

Kelly and the Three-toed Horse
Imperial Kelly
Kelly Blue
Yellowstone Kelly

The Tumbler

The Tumbler

PETER BOWEN

ST. MARTIN'S MINOTAUR
NEW YORK

www.minotaurbooks.com

Library of Congress Cataloging-in-Publication Data

Bowen, Peter, 1945–
    The tumbler : a Gabriel Du Pré mystery /Peter Bowen.—1st ed.
        p. cm.
    ISBN 0-312-27733-4
    EAN 978-0312-27733-8
    1. Du Pré, Gabriel (Fictitious character)—Fiction. 2. Lewis, Meriwether, 1774–1809—Diaries—Fiction. 3. Clark, William, 1770–1838—Diaries—Fiction. 4. Manuscripts—Collectors and collecting—Fiction. 5. Sheriffs—Fiction. 6. Montana—Fiction. I. Title.

PS3552.O866T86 2004
813'.54—dc22

                                                    2003058537

First Edition: April 2004

10   9   8   7   6   5   4   3   2   1

For Nancy and
Prince Henry the Laminator

Gabriel Du Pré's Toussaint

GABRIEL DU PRÉ—Metis fiddler, retired brand inspector, solver of puzzles

MADELAINE PLACQUEMINES—Gabriel's woman, children Robert and Thierry (away in Marines) and Lourdes (studying art in Chicago)

JACQUELINE FORTIER—m. Raymond Fortier, twelve children, Du Pré's daughter

MARIA DU PRÉ—Du Pré's daughter, studying overseas

BART FASCELLI—very rich neighbor, alcoholic, runs earthmoving business, money out of Chicago

CHARLES FOOTE—lawyer, troubleshooter for Bart, manages Fascelli empire

BENETSEE—ancient medicine person, mysterious, always been around

BENNY KLEIN—sheriff

SUSAN KLEIN—former schoolteacher, now owns and runs Toussaint Saloon

HARVEY WALLACE—Blackfoot Indian and FBI agent, lives in Washington D.C.

RIPPER—Charles Van Dusen, young agent, mad duck

PALLAS FORTIER—Daughter of Jacqueline and Raymond, genius, determined to marry Ripper, if necessary marry his dead body

SAMANTHA PIDGEON—incredibly beautiful and brainy serial killer expert works for FBI, Redbone girl from California

FATHER VAN DEN HEUVEL—Belgian Jesuit, pastor of little Catholic church in Toussaint, physically very inept

JACQUELINE'S CHILDREN—Alcide, Pallas, Lourdes, Marisa & Berne (twins), Hervé Nepthele, Marie and Barbara (twins), Armand, Gabriel, Colette

PELON—apprentice to Benetsee, often far away on some mysterious business

The Tumbler

CHAPTER

1

"She was some pissed," said Bassman. He looked carefully at the bullet holes in the rear window of his van. "Shit, I know she can shoot that good, maybe I am nicer to her."

"You are lucky," said Madelaine, "you don't get one of them the back of the head."

"Cheap-ass little twenty-five," said Bassman. "She shot me that two times. Gun jammed. She is messing, the slide, think I am going to hit her. Me, I am taking out my jackknife, I open the blade, dig out them two slugs are stuck in my arm. They don't even go in so far."

Bassman held out his left forearm. There were two round scabs on the side of his elbow.

Du Pré snorted.

Bassman, he thought, him, always got that burlap blonde girlfriend, all look the same from the neck down. Big tits, round ass. Neck up they all got mean eyes. I live with that Bassman, I am probably mean, too.

They were standing out in front of the Toussaint Saloon, and it was a miserable gray April day, dead sky, old leaves and grass, and plenty of dog turds.

"So maybe she is coming after you?" said Madelaine. "You fill them women that true love, Bassman."

"Yah," said Bassman, "maybe she does, you know. She got a temper, that one. I give it some time, she start shooting at someone else maybe."

We go and play the roadhouse down the Missouri, thought Du Pré, make that good music, Bassman have another burlap blonde by the second set tomorrow night. Latest he will have her then.

Bassman went in to get another beer. The giant joint he had been smoking had dried his throat.

"You got maybe one cousin is not crazy?" said Madelaine.

Du Pré shook his head.

"Me, either," said Madelaine. "All of them, crazy."

Du Pré laughed and he put his arm around her.

The air smelled of snow.

The clouds broke and the Wolf Mountains blazed white in the sun.

"Maybe we don' burn up this year," said Madelaine.

Du Pré shrugged.

Maybe.

It is very dry here still. I don't see it so dry so deep, a long time. Bart, he is digging a coffer slot for a little dam, he says he never hit the water table, goes down twenty feet. In the bottom of a coulee.

Bassman came back out, belching. He had a huge can of beer, blue and gold, in his hand.

"Australia," he said, holding up the can. "We maybe move there, yes?"

Madelaine snorted.

"Long way to go, a beer," she said.

"Some people," said Bassman, "they see the Virgin Mary, a tortilla or maybe a birthmark, their kid's ass, me, I see this. I maybe make a pilgrimage."

Father Van Den Heuvel came out of the tiny white Catholic church. He waved and he tripped over something in the yard. He fell on his hands, bounced up, and went on.

The big Jesuit got in his ratty old Ford and he started it and he drove away.

"Least him, don't shut his head in the car door this time," said Madelaine.

"Him shut his head, the car door?" said Bassman.

"Knocked cold," said Madelaine.

"I never hear that before," said Bassman.

"Stay a week," said Du Pré. "You see that, couple times."

Bart drove up in his pickup. He got out and came over to them. He looked tired, and his clothes were caked with clay.

"Water down pret' far," said Du Pré.

"Way down," said Bart.

"Bad summer," said Madelaine. "Or maybe it rain."

"Julie's coming," said Bart.

"You got a new girlfriend," said Madelaine. "Ver' good."

"No," said Bart, "I got a niece. My sister Angela's kid. Angie is a counselor in Portland."

Madelaine nodded.

"OK," she said.

Du Pré looked at his friend. Bart's family had been blown apart by money and alcohol. So had Bart. He was rich, and he dug holes, and he liked it.

"Trouble?" said Madelaine.

Bart nodded.

"Trouble," he said.

Madelaine went to him. She kissed him on the cheek.

"It be OK," she said. "Now, you maybe come along hear some good music."

Bart shook his head.

"I got to have that dam done tomorrow," he said. "I just came in to get a hamburger and check my messages."

"OK," said Bassman, "we got some miles maybe."

"Take a long time you piss so much," said Madelaine.

The three of them got into Bassman's van. It was a dope crib on wheels, with two small refrigerators and three captain's chairs and a thick sweet fug of marijuana in the air.

"Jesus," said Madelaine. "I get high just sitting in here."

"Yeah," said Bassman, starting the engine, "nice, ain't it."

For all his bad habits, Bassman was a very good driver. He was

3

soon rocketing down the highway. He saw a truck coming and he slowed down so he wouldn't meet it on the narrow bridge over Cooper's Creek.

"So you never been there to play before, Du Pré?" said Bassman.

"*Non*," said Du Pré, "that roadhouse it is closed for years, then it is bought, new people. Grand opening."

"Moon of Dog Turds," said Bassman. "These people are what? Yuppies come to Montana, open this fancy restaurant. Bad food cost a lot of money. I go one of them. All they got, goddamned *noodles*."

Madelaine laughed.

"Noodles," said Bassman again.

Du Pré slipped his flask out of his bag. He had some good bourbon whiskey. He rolled a cigarette.

"Pink wine the fridge," said Bassman.

"*Non*," said Madelaine, "too early."

"Too bad, Talley," said Bassman.

Du Pré nodded. Poor Talley, born with an open spine, lived for thirty-six years, most of the time infected, gets an infection they can do nothing for.

"Hell of an accordion player," said Bassman.

"He was that," said Du Pré. He lit his cigarette and he passed it to Madelaine. She took one long drag and gave it back.

"Him just go like that," said Madelaine. "I am talking to him, the telephone one day, I call back two days later he is dead."

Poor Talley, crippled, has to use crutches, plays hell out of that accordion.

Bassman got the van up to eighty-five and he kept it there.

Montana, you go fifty-five you never get anywhere, Du Pré thought. When you do get someplace, it is North Dakota.

"This girlfriend, she knows you are playing here?" said Madelaine.

"Maybe," said Bassman. "She don't got a car, though."

"What you do she shows up?" said Madelaine.

"Me, I am a brave Métis," said Bassman. "I run like hell, what I do, I see that damn woman."

"This is that Charmayne?" said Madelaine.

"*Non*," said Bassman, "this is Kim. Charmayne, she was maybe a year ago, little more."

"Ah," said Madelaine, "but they look like each other."

"Yah," said Bassman.

"All the time blondes," said Madelaine.

"White bread," said Bassman, "you know."

Du Pré laughed.

Poor Talley, he thought.

Good man.

Bassman came to the highway that went south toward the Missouri. He looked both ways and he pulled out and accelerated.

Big fat wet flakes of snow started to fall.

The snow got thicker.

I play a song, maybe two, tonight for Talley, thought Du Pré.

CHAPTER

2

"Jesus," said Bassman.

"Christ," said Du Pré.

"Well," said Madelaine, "it *is* pretty."

They were looking at what had been the old roadhouse, once a typical Great Plains hovel, weatherproof, warm in winter, racked in the frame, covered with plywood that bore a fading coat of cheap red paint, and the marks of drunken handiwork.

The new building was made of logs.

"Mahogany, maybe?" said Bassman.

"Jesus," said Du Pré, "maybe rosewood."

"It is *pretty!*" said Madelaine.

There were two long sparkling picture windows in the front, one on each side of the double doors.

"How long them last?" said Bassman.

"Maybe tonight," said Du Pré. "It is Friday."

"Things drunkest out Friday night," said Bassman.

"OK," said Madelaine, "so they are dumb windows. It is easy. Guys get thrown through them, they put in small ones, too small to throw anybody through."

"They are not from here," said Bassman. He looked over at a shiny dark green SUV parked beside the mailbox at the end of the ornamental hitching rail.

"Those are cedar shakes," said Du Pré, squinting at the roof.

"Those are in fucking Fargo first time the wind blows," said Bassman.

"I leave you two Laurel and Hardy here," said Madelaine. "I go in, I have a nice glass, pink wine, I say, 'The band is out in the van, they are shooting up, will be right in.'"

Du Pré sighed.

"This thing it belongs in Bozeman maybe," he said. Bozeman was full of buildings as pretty as the redone roadhouse.

Madelaine opened the van door.

"Wipe your feet, you go in," she said.

"Yeah, mom!" said Bassman and Du Pré.

Madelaine stepped up on the long porch that went the entire length of the front of the building. She pulled on the front door and it swung slowly open.

"I don't got a tie," said Bassman.

"You are wearing shoes," said Du Pré. "Maybe they let you come in."

"Jesus," said Bassman, "I liked that old place."

Du Pré nodded.

"Well," he said, "we go say hello. This woman, she sounds very nice on the telephone."

They got out and they went up the front steps and they pulled open a door apiece and they went in.

The place was lovely.

Nice wooden chairs. Little tables.

No moldy moose heads.

Real paintings on the walls.

The backbar was new, and had been bought for a whole lot of money from some old saloon. There was a vast mirror in the center.

"Last maybe tonight," said Bassman, nodding at the silvered glass. "Maybe a month even, then a stool goes through it."

Du Pré nodded.

Madelaine was talking to a pretty young woman, blond and scrubbed, who had her hair in a thick plait down her back. The two of them were laughing.

Du Pré and Bassman walked on over.

"This is Du Pré," said Madelaine, "that is Bassman. This is Carol Canning. She owns the place."

"Me and Rob," she said. "He went to get some things we thought we might need."

Du Pré smiled and he shook her hand across the bar. He looked up and down it.

Some ashtrays, Du Pré thought, first hopeful sign I am seeing.

He rolled a smoke and he lit it and he blew out the tobacco.

Carol got an ashtray from under the bartop and she put it in front of him.

"Ditch?" she said.

"She studying on our language," said Bassman, grinning. "Him have one, me, too."

Carol made them quickly. One splash glop splash bourbon over ice tap water.

Du Pré nodded and he took his drink.

Carol set the other in front of Bassman.

"I love it here," said Carol. "We wanted to move to the real West. We found this place. I worked for six months at a roadhouse, and Rob went to work for a rancher. We learned a lot."

Du Pré nodded.

"These places are community centers," said Carol, "more even than they are saloons."

Bassman and Madelaine and Du Pré nodded.

"Everything we have is in this place," said Carol. "We're going to make a go of it."

Bassman got up and he went out the front door.

His van's sliding door opened and closed.

A tall young man in jeans and boots came in carrying a big box of groceries. He set them on the bartop and he came over to Du Pré and Madelaine.

"I'm Rob," he said, "Mr. Du Pré, and . . ."

"Madelaine," said Madelaine.

He shook their hands and grinned and he went back out. Carol took the box in the back.

Rob came in again, with another huge box.

"You want some help?" said Du Pré.

"Appreciate," said Rob.

They went out together.

"I really like the people here," said Carol. "They are so helpful and courteous. I thought we would be resented, you know, god-damned flatlanders. So before we came we both went through the EMT course and got certified and Rob is part of the volunteer fire department."

Madelaine nodded.

"There's more traffic on the road now," said Carol. "We put in a good big truck parking lot, for the haulers."

Rob and Du Pré came in and they went round the end of the bar with the boxes.

"I think we got everything covered," said Carol. "Rob will tend bar tonight while I cook and we have four waitresses."

Madelaine nodded.

"We put up posters all over," said Carol. "Grand opening."

Madelaine nodded.

"Which roadhouse you work at?" she said.

"Tucker's," said Carol, "down by Forsyth."

Madelaine shook her head.

"Don't know that one," she said. "That smells good." A waft of air had come out of the kitchen.

"It was a real education," said Carol.

Madelaine nodded.

"Just you in the kitchen, maybe?" she said.

Carol nodded. "It'll be hard," she said.

"Well," said Madelaine, "you need help I help you."

"Thanks," said Carol.

Bassman opened the door and he rolled in his big amplifier. He looked round for the stage, and saw it at the far side of the room. The wheels went *scritch scritch* on the puncheon floor.

Du Pré went to help him. His hat brushed a wagon wheel chandelier. He looked up at it. He shook his head.

"Little blisters be hanging from that like apes," said Bassman, watching the wagon wheel rock gently.

Du Pré nodded.

"Maybe," said Du Pré, "there have been lots, Mormons move here or something."

"They don't go to bars," said Bassman.

Du Pré nodded.

"These are nice people," said Bassman.

Du Pré nodded.

"We make some, that good music," said Bassman.

"Wish Talley was here," said Du Pré.

Somebody came in the door.

"Père Godin!" said Madelaine, running to the old scoundrel.

Some Turtle Mountain people were with him.

"Ah," said Du Pré.

Père Godin was a very good accordion player.

"We play some for Talley, him," said Bassman.

Du Pré nodded.

CHAPTER

3

The roadhouse was full of people. They could sit and stand in comfort, but if many more came in it would start to get difficult to move.

Père Godin was riffing notes on his accordion. The old man was spry and quick, and the notes stabbed and jabbed along the melody.

Du Pré stood back, marking time, while Bassman thumped away, putting a floor under Père Godin's runs. Du Pré stepped forward and he slid in to the melody and Père Godin stepped back.

Du Pré stood at the mike and he began to sing.

> *Pull that paddle long time to go*
> *Madelaine I love her so*
> *Pull on that rope, my Madelaine*
> *And I come home to you . . .*

Some older couples were two-stepping on the little dance floor.

A young boy leaped up and grabbed the wagon wheel and he hung there for a moment until his mother snapped at him to get the hell down.

Du Pré and Bassman and Père Godin played for another twenty minutes and then they took a break.

The crowd went to talking to one another. There were all sorts of people in the room, young and old, families, single people, and many children.

The four waitresses were carrying armloads of plates. People had been eating a lot of beef.

Madelaine was pulling beers and pouring shots and mixing drinks, and so was Rob. People were three deep at the bar getting booze after the music stopped.

Du Pré and Bassman and Père Godin waited until the crowd thinned, and then they went to the end of the bar. Madelaine bustled down with three ditchwater highballs and she set them down and she went back to work.

The three musicians drank.

By the time they had drained their glasses Madelaine was back with three more. She set them down and was gone again.

Carol came out of the kitchen, looking sweaty and exhausted. She drank three tall glasses of water very quickly and she went back to the kitchen.

The bar crowd had thinned out and Madelaine waved at Du Pré and she went back to the kitchen, too.

Rob finished the last pulls and he looked up and down the bar and then he came down to Du Pré and Bassman and Père Godin.

"Great music," he said, "wonderful. Madelaine is even more wonderful. God, we'd have sunk without her." He looked at the crowd in the room.

Du Pré laughed.

"More people than we thought would come," said Rob.

"They like you," said Du Pré.

A couple of young hands went out the side door. Friends followed them prepared to slap the victor on his back and carry the vanquished to his truck until he woke up.

Families with young children began to leave, hugging parents and kin, and several tables opened up. No one went to them right away, so the rush was over at last.

Madelaine came back out of the kitchen.

"They are down to the last half of one prime ribs," she said. "It was a pret' good guess."

Du Pré nodded. Nice crowd, nice place. Wonder how long them picture windows will last.

The side door opened and a sound of cheering came in.

"Punchin' the spots off each other," said an old rancher bellied up to the bar. "Them youngsters been at it a while now. Must be about evenly matched."

Père Godin wandered off to charm a woman someplace.

Old bastard, him got what, sixty kids I hear? Half of Manitoba is Père Godin's.

"I work real hard," said Bassman, "I maybe fuck one woman for his ten."

Du Pré laughed. Madelaine had said once Père Godin loved women and they could tell.

Old goat.

Highly successful old goat.

Père Godin was sitting with a pretty lady at a small table off in a corner. He said something and she laughed.

"Sixty-four," said Madelaine, glancing at him.

"Ah?" said Du Pré.

"Him got sixty-three kids," said Madelaine, "and believe me, that is one done deal over there, the table."

Bassman and Du Pré laughed.

They wandered back up to the stage and Du Pré tuned his fiddle and he started *Baptiste's Lament.*

Black water, black forest, big canoes full of bales of pelts.

Long time gone.

Père Godin played some Cajun accordion. He had children down in Louisiana, too. His accordion and charm carried him far.

The woman he had been talking to was looking at Père Godin with adoring eyes. He looked at her while his accordion played a song of love.

Du Pré stepped in before the woman fell off her chair.

He played a very old reel, one that Du Pré's father, Catfoot, had said went all the way back to Brittany.

Them people, Catfoot had said, they dance this there, they dance this on the decks, their little fishing boats, they dance this on the shore, Gulf of St. Lawrence, dance it on buffalo hide pegged to the ground, here. Long time gone.

The tune was so old and rare that people stopped talking so they could listen closely. It spoke to the blood.

Du Pré ended the reel with the long, lonely, wavering high F.

The crowd clapped and clapped and cheered and whistled. A man began to pass his hat around and people dropped money in it.

Bassman began to play a melody on his bass, his moment at the front of the stage. He stood lazily, loosely, while he coaxed notes from his fretless electric bass. His strong fingers pressed and pulled the strings.

There was humor and self-mockery in the music, and people grinned.

Du Pré looked at his sideman, nodding at tempo.

Du Pré was looking at Bassman when he saw Bassman's eyes widen, and Du Pré turned and he looked at the woman stalking toward the stage.

Must be that Kim, and she had a little chrome-plated gun in her hand.

Bassman backed away.

Kim kept coming.

She fired the pistol and Bassman's bass took a hit.

Bassman shrugged out of the strap and he dropped the bass and he made time for the side door and he dove through it just as some poor person was coming in. Bassman went right over the top of him.

Kim raced after him, her tight pants and high heels slowing her some.

When she got to the door, she fired again.

Then she went through.

It had happened fast, and people weren't really sure that they had seen what they had seen.

Bassman's wounded bass buzzed on the floor.

Du Pré went to the amplifier and he turned the knob. He pulled the cord that led to the bass out of its socket.

Another couple of pops outside.

Rob came running up.

"Jesus!" he said, "are you OK?"

Du Pré looked past him. Madelaine was wrestling, sort of, with Carol.

Du Pré and Rob ran back to the bar.

"Call 911!" Carol shrieked.

"Non!" said Madelaine.

They each had hold of the telephone.

"She tried to kill him!" Carol howled.

"Non!" said Madelaine, "leave it be. That little damn gun can't kill no more than a gopher, can't hit anything with it anyway."

Carol stopped struggling.

"You're sure," she said.

Madelaine nodded.

"Was that his girlfriend?" said Carol.

Madelaine shrugged.

"One of them maybe," she said.

"She was shooting at him!" said Carol.

"She hit the damn bass," said Du Pré. "Wound it good, too."

"You don't think this is something I should call the sheriff about?" said Carol.

Madelaine grinned.

"True love," she said, "sometimes it is a hard thing."

Another couple of pops sounded outside.

CHAPTER 4

Père Godin carried the last of Bassman's things to the shed in back of Madelaine's house.

The Turtle Mountain people were in the kitchen having a big breakfast.

"That Bassman," said Du Pré, "that son of a bitch, him, he takes off, leaves his shit."

"She is shooting at him," said Père Godin.

"She is not hitting him," said Du Pré.

"Maybe," said Père Godin, "Bassman, him, he is worried she is a bad shot, maybe hit him not mean to."

"I hope she shoots him," said Du Pré.

"Him good bass player," said Père Godin. "They are all crazy. Fiddler too."

Du Pré grinned.

"Accordion players," he said.

The Turtle Mountain people came out and they all hugged Du Pré and they got in their old cars. They drove off with Père Godin waving from the back seat of the Chevrolet.

Madelaine put her hand on Du Pré's shoulder.

"Good music," she said. "Ver' good music, though not so good after Bassman lights out. Him, him think with his dick."

Du Pré nodded.

"They are fucking like minks now," said Madelaine. "You will see."

Du Pré snorted.

"You got that court case Billings tomorrow," said Madelaine. "Meet them lawyer tonight you remember."

Du Pré nodded.

"Those damn journals," said Madelaine, "big fight. You find them they are yours, yes?"

Du Pré laughed. The lost journals of William Clark, cached on the way back home after the Corps of Discovery had gone all of the way to the Pacific Ocean.

"I go and find Benetsee," said Du Pré.

He went to his old police cruiser, which still had a working light bar and siren. The decals had been taken off the sides.

He drove out of town and up the long bench road to the west and down to the little valley where Benetsee's cabin was, on a low shoulder of land above Cooper's Creek.

There was smoke coming from the chimney.

Du Pré drove up the winding rutted track and he parked in the dead weeds.

Snow, mud, dust, Du Pré thought, Montana seasons.

Du Pré stepped up on the porch, and he waited until the door swung open and he went on in.

The old man smiled, his wizened weathered face like a ball of twine with sparkling black eyes in it.

I see him he is smaller each time a little, Du Pré thought.

The cabin was very warm. There was a heavy smell. A spice. Cardamom.

Du Pré nodded and he went back out to the cruiser and he opened the trunk and he got out a jug of the fizzy wine Benetsee liked. Madelaine had left a small plastic bag of venison and plum stew on the seat. Du Pré took that, too.

The old man was waiting on the porch when Du Pré came back. He had a clean quart jar in his hand. Du Pré filled the jar with wine and the old man drank it down slowly and steadily.

"I got to go, Billings," said Du Pré. "That Lewis and Clark stuff we find. The government is suing me."

Benetsee held out the jar and Du Pré poured. He rolled the old man a cigarette and he lit it and he passed it to him.

"Pret' fancy," said Benetsee. "You must be ver' big man, have a government sue you, Du Pré."

"Pain in the ass," said Du Pré.

"Government," said Benetsee, shrugging.

"That stuff," said Du Pré, "I lose, don't give it to them, they will throw me in jail."

Benetsee nodded.

"You been in jail," he said. "It is not so bad."

Du Pré looked at him.

"I don' need your bullshit now, old man, this is not a joke," said Du Pré.

"Hee," said Benetsee, "Ever'thing is a joke, Du Pré, even death, him."

Du Pré nodded. He rolled himself a cigarette.

"OK," said Du Pré, "I get bail maybe, have a little time, me, before they throw me in the can. So I come here, shoot you, make myself feel better."

"Sure," said Benetsee, "that Du Pré, I say, him, ver' smart."

Du Pré sighed.

"OK," he said, "old man, what I do here?"

"I go with you," said Benetsee.

"OK," said Du Pré. "I say the judge, here is old fart got that stuff you want. So throw him in jail, yes."

"Ah," said Benetsee, "good wine."

The old man went inside and Du Pré could hear him rummaging around. He came out in a moment with a blue nylon backpack.

"OK," said Benetsee, "we go now, yes."

Du Pré looked at him.

"You are coming with me?" he said.

Benetsee nodded.

"Good," said Du Pré, "they hang us both then."

"Good thing," said Benetsee, "have company."

"Hang on the rope there," said Du Pré, "ver' lucky me."

Benetsee patted him on the knee.

"We just go," he said, "that Billings."

Du Pré nodded.

"OK," he said, "mess on the front seat, you ride in back?"

He got in and opened the rear door for Benetsee. The cruiser still had the cage wire behind the front seat and no handles on the inside of the rear doors.

Du Pré got in and he pulled the flask from under the seat and he had some whiskey and then he rolled a smoke and he lit it. He started the cruiser's big engine and he backed around and went down the track.

When he got to the county road, he turned left instead of right.

"Billings, that way," said Benetsee.

"Madelaine, that way," said Du Pré.

"You are a bastard, Du Pré," said Benetsee.

Du Pré drove to Toussaint, and he parked in front of the house.

He got out.

Madelaine stood in the open front door.

"Benetsee, him want to go with me," said Du Pré.

"OK," said Madelaine, "me, I think I see."

"Big trial," said Du Pré. "Good witness him."

"Smells bad, though," said Madelaine. She wiped her hands on her apron and she came down the steps and out to the car.

Benetsee sat like stone in the prisoner's cage.

"Old man!" said Madelaine, "you need, that bath! Clean clothes."

"You," said Benetsee, smiling at Du Pré, "me, I am behind you, walking ver' softly, like death."

"Old man," said Madelaine, "in the goddamn house, the shower. I see about clothes for you, yes."

Du Pré opened the door.

"Son of bitch," said Benetsee pleasantly, "you, him."

Du Pré nodded.

"It is worth it, die now," he said.

Benetsee went up the walk and inside.

Madelaine grinned at Du Pré.

"Old fart," she said, "fix him, yes, me. I will make him wear a tie."

19

Du Pré roared.

He reached in to the back of the car and he got the blue nylon backpack.

Madelaine took it. She frowned as she felt the stuff inside.

She unzipped the bag.

Some underwear made of doeskin. Fringed pants of deerhide. A pair of moccasins with Nez Percé beadwork on them. And a long fringed shirt at the bottom. Madelaine pulled it out and she unfolded it.

The shirt was of pale tan deerskin. It had many designs done on the yoke and chest in porcupine quills dyed with roots pounded and boiled, the old way.

A single blue star on the back, with six points.

"This is ver' beautiful stuff, Du Pré," said Madelaine.

Du Pré nodded.

"Him always know everything," said Du Pré.

"Get you drive here his bath," said Madelaine.

"Yes," said Du Pré.

CHAPTER

5

The lawyer was waiting for Du Pré in the hall. The Federal Building had long corridors that smelled of polish. Muted voices far away decided fates.

Benetsee padded along beside Du Pré, his moccasined feet making slip slip slip noises on the buffed poured stone.

"Massingham," said the lawyer. He held out a huge beefy hand and Du Pré shook it. He offered it to Benetsee and the old man waved it away like it was a fly.

The lawyer shrugged.

"We have appealed," he said, "I think you know. This hearing is to show cause why you have not turned over the artifacts pending the outcome."

Du Pré nodded.

"Him not turning them over," said Benetsee, "him not have them. They belong, his daughter, me. I have them, Du Pré does not know where they are hidden. Me, I know."

The lawyer looked at Du Pré, who nodded.

"You really don't know, do you," said the lawyer.

Du Pré shook his head.

"Christ," said the lawyer, "this judge may not like that."

"I talk to him," said Benetsee.

"You have no standing at the moment, sir," said the lawyer.

"I am standing, here," said Benetsee. He turned to Du Pré.

He came close.

"You go have nice drink someplace," said Benetsee. "I take care of this chickenshit."

Du Pré laughed.

The lawyer looked at the ceiling.

"Christ," he said.

"I come," said Du Pré, "him, Benetsee, he needs to speak."

The lawyer sighed.

"We'll see what the judge says," he said.

"Judge, him talk to me," said Benetsee.

The lawyer threw up his hands. He looked at his thick gold watch.

"Down here," he said.

He held the door for Du Pré and the old man and just beyond it was a guard and a metal detector. The lawyer handed over his briefcase and the guard peered into it and he set it on the other side of the metal frame. The lawyer handed the watch to the guard and he went through the detector and the guard gave him the watch.

Du Pré pulled the multitool from its sheath and he handed it to the guard and he walked through the metal detector. The dingus buzzed.

The guard motioned him to come back.

Du Pré sighed.

"The belt buckle," said the guard.

Du Pré took off the belt with the heavy oval buckle and he gave it to the guard.

He walked through the metal detector and it buzzed.

Du Pré took out his pocketknife and all the change he had and he gave them to the guard and he walked through the metal detector.

It buzzed.

Benetsee laughed.

Du Pré spread his hands.

"You got any metal in you?" said the guard. "Steel pins, surgical hardware?"

Du Pré shook his head.

"Saw off his dick," said Benetsee.

The guard looked at the old man.

"What?" he said.

Benetsee waved at the metal detector and he walked through it and he motioned for Du Pré to come along and he walked through and the thing was silent.

The guard looked at the old man.

Benetsee ignored him.

The metal detector began to crackle and buzz. It got louder and louder.

The guard looked at it and he frowned.

There were about twenty people in the courtroom. Most of them were journalists, crouched over their notebooks.

The two federal attorneys at their table looked up and nodded at Du Pré's lawyer. They looked long and hard at Benetsee. The old man stood just in front of the two tables.

"All rise!" said the bailiff.

Everyone stood. The young judge came through the drapes and he went to his seat and he sat and nodded at the court.

The bailiff went to Benetsee and he whispered something to him.

Benetsee ignored him.

The judge was trying not to notice the old man, who, in his beads and quills and buckskins, was very hard to miss.

The bailiff motioned to some guards at the back of the room.

The guards began to walk toward the bailiff and the old man who would not move.

The guards took hold of Benetsee's arms.

They began to pull the old man away.

Benetsee did not move.

The guards looked at each other, puzzled.

They took better stances and they pulled.

Benetsee did not move.

The metal detector began to crackle and buzz even louder than it had.

The security guard reached down and the metal detector went silent.

There were three windows on the east wall of the room, high ones, open on their pivots, so that the metal and glass window was set at about a forty-five-degree angle from level.

Du Pré saw a shadow.

A huge golden eagle landed at the window, grabbing the frame in its yellow talons. The big bird folded its wings and looked calmly down into the room.

"Judge Clemens," said one of the government attorneys, "I move—"

The judge waved at him.

"Sir," he said, looking at Benetsee, "I have heard of you. Now, I think you have something to say to the court, and of course you may."

"Your honor!" said the federal attorney.

"Us, only," said Benetsee.

The judge looked at the old man.

"Bailiff," he said, "please clear the courtroom."

"Your honor!" said the federal attorney.

"This is an ex parte hearing," said the judge.

"This is irregular," said the federal attorney.

"Tell ya what, Ralph," said the judge, "you get an eagle to come and sit on the window up there and I'll grant you your own ex parte. Until then, get your ass out of here. Miss Held . . ."

The court reporter looked up.

"Note I told Ralph to get his ass out of here," said the judge.

"Yes, your honor," said the reporter.

The bailiff was herding journalists and lawyers out the doors.

Du Pré went, along with his attorney.

"Mr. Benetsee," said the judge, "could I ask you a favor? I do need a record of this. May Miss Held stay?"

"Yah," said Benetsee.

The crowd out in the hall was joined by the bailiff, who shut the doors and stood in front of them.

The federal attorneys and Massingham were standing together saying things like *I don't believe this.*

"Who is that old Indian, I mean Native American?" said a woman to Du Pré. She had a tape recorder on her purse.

"Him Indian," said Du Pré, "them Native Americans teach writing at colleges. He is Indian."

"What kind of Indian?" said the woman.

"Pain-in-the-ass Indian," said Du Pré.

"Does he have a pet eagle?" she said.

Du Pré shook his head.

The security guard's radio squawked.

". . . There's three coyotes in the parking lot . . . We've called Animal Control . . . Don't let anyone leave the building. They may be rabid."

Du Pré laughed.

The woman reporter came close.

"I want to talk to that old man," she said.

"*Non,*" said Du Pré, "you do not, believe me."

"What is going on in there?" said one of the journalists.

". . . Six coyotes in the parking lot now . . ." said the radio.

CHAPTER

6

"The judge granted a continuance," said Massingham. "That gives us another six months."

Du Pré nodded.

They were seated at a big round table in a fancy restaurant. The waitresses all wore black bodices and flaring skirts. The food was awful.

Du Pré ate a little more of his fruity goulash and he had some beer.

"Where did Benetsee go?" said Massingham. "I thought he rode down here with you."

"Him come and go," said Du Pré.

Old piece of shit turn into an eagle and fly home, Du Pré thought, it is faster and makes me crazy, too.

"He spoke with the judge for ten minutes," said Massingham, "and he must have gone out through the judge's chambers."

Massingham ate a chunk of his heavy German food.

Du Pré looked at his goulash.

I am in the army, Germany, he thought, I eat this crap, wonder why we don't just shoot them all. Crime against humanity, this food.

"Good god," said Massingham. He looked toward the entrance.

The judge and Benetsee were standing there, and then the hostess took them to a table over by the window. Diners looked up from their plates and marveled at the little old man in his buckskins.

Massingham sighed.

"That old fellow has a considerable moral force," he said, "but as your attorney, I really would appreciate knowing what is going on. If you find out, do let me know."

Du Pré nodded.

"You win," he said to the goulash, and he got up.

He shook Massingham's hand and he went over to the table where the judge and the medicine person were going to have lunch.

The judge looked up and he nodded.

"Old man," said Du Pré, "I, me, am about to maybe go, jail, and I do not want to do that."

Benetsee grinned.

"Builds character," said Benetsee. "Food got lots, vitamins, I hear."

The judge began to laugh.

"Goddamn it," said Du Pré. "This is not funny."

"You are whining," said Benetsee. "Sit down and shut up. Me, judge here, having lunch, discussing, white men call it."

Du Pré pulled out the faux chair and he sat down.

"How long this take, anyway?" said Du Pré.

Benetsee looked at him.

"You got your job," he said. "Don't got to complain so much. We are here until we are done. Then you drive me home maybe."

Du Pré nodded. He wanted a smoke but not before the others at the table ate.

The barmaid came.

"Big whiskey," said Du Pré.

"Menu?" she said.

"*Non*," said Du Pré.

She went away.

The judge steepled his fingers, his elbows on the thick white tablecloth.

"Benetsee tells me," he said, "that the lost journals and so forth may be returned in six months but for now they figure in another case which has precedence."

Du Pré looked at the old man.

"Nineteen eleven," said Benetsee.

Du Pré looked at the floor.

Nineteen eleven. Black Jack Pershing, some soldiers, round up the Métis don't got papers, prove they are American, put four hundred, boxcars. It is the winter, cold, send them to Red River country, North Dakota, drive them north to the Canada border. Eighty-three people die, old people, children, from the cold.

"I did not know," said the judge.

"Two Métis corpses they are not buried," said Benetsee. "They are taken, that Washington, D.C. Made into skeletons. Now they are in boxes there. They got to come back."

"The great age of grave robbing," said the judge. "Called anthropology then and now."

Du Pré looked at Benetsee.

"This is old bones?" he said.

Benetsee looked sad for a moment and then he smiled.

"Want their bones back home, them," he said.

"Ah," said Du Pré. Souls, ghosts, speak to Benetsee, that is it.

Bring us home.

The barmaid brought Du Pré's whiskey.

Du Pré sipped it.

"Who these people are?" he said to Benetsee.

"Métis want to come home," said Benetsee. And he grinned. He drank some white wine from his tulip glass.

Du Pré shrugged.

This is not all the story, he thought. I find the rest in time.

The judge leaned back and let the waitress set down his platter.

Benetsee did the same.

Pork tenderloin on sauerkraut.

"I'm not certain," said the judge, "just what case Benetsee means. My staff is researching it."

Benetsee was eating and he didn't reply.

"As soon as we rose to go in the courtroom," said the judge, "the eagle left and the coyotes were gone, I was told, just like that. They were sitting like statues, looking up at the eagle. And then they were gone, just like that."

Du Pré nodded.

"Mister Benetsee?" said the judge.

"Mister is whiteman talk," said Benetsee. "I am Benetsee."

"So you are," said the judge. "I don't mean to be rude, but . . . I would like to ask Mr. Du Pré some questions, and don't wish to have you feel I am doing so in front of you. Some of them concern you."

"Him don't know gopher fart's worth about anything," said Benetsee. "I got to waste my time with him. You want to, go ahead."

Du Pré laughed.

"If this indeed is about the return of some bones stolen by those charming people whose gross racism excused the ransacking of graves and the stealing of corpses, back then," said the judge, "and there is another case, it is still a most peculiar demand. It smells of extortion, actually. I wonder if I could possibly make any sense of this in terms of the law."

Benetsee looked up from his plate.

"You don't got to," he said, "it is all right."

"I was not about to throw an aged and holy person in the slam," said the judge. "God alone knows how many damn coyotes that would have brought into town."

Du Pré nodded.

"Them ain't too bad," he said, "but them skunks, they are."

"Skunks," said the judge.

Benetsee was wolfing down his pork tenderloin.

"Have you known Benetsee for a long time?" said the judge.

"Too long," said Du Pré. "I will shoot him just as soon as we are past, city limits."

The judge roared with laughter.

"Do you know what this is about?" said the judge.

Du Pré shook his head.

"What then should I do?" said the judge.

Du Pré sighed.

"Medicine people," he said, "they maybe do things, call it magic maybe, but . . . they cannot do it for evil, or to feed their own greed."

The judge looked intently at Du Pré.

"You believe Benetsee can perform . . . magic?" said the judge.

"Check your window," said Du Pré. "Got eagle shit on it. Eagle, they eat so much they shit all the time."

The judge nodded.

"But you say if . . . a medicine person does anything . . . immoral . . . they lose their powers," said the judge.

Du Pré nodded.

"God," said the judge, "we could use that in Washington, D.C."

Du Pré laughed.

Benetsee ate. He had some more white wine.

"Damn it," said the judge, "something will have to be done within six months."

Du Pré nodded.

"You two," said Benetsee, "worry too much. You eat, drink. It is fine, you know."

"What other case do these artifacts figure in, really?" said the judge.

"Him smarter than you," said Benetsee, looking at Du Pré.

The judge threw up his hands.

"Case hasn't happened yet," said Benetsee. "You two, worry too much."

CHAPTER

7

"Nice new hole there," said Du Pré, squinting at the back window of Bassman's van.

Bassman set the heavy amplifier in the back of the van and he shoved it in to the wheel blocks.

"Yah," he said. "Another, the front there. Good thing you are not sitting, the passenger seat."

Du Pré looked through the van and he saw the hole in the windshield. It was about neck high for a passenger.

"You got any holes?" said Du Pré.

"Bunch of them," said Bassman. "Born with them all. Kim didn't add none."

"She is still gunning for you?" said Du Pré.

"I take the gun away," said Bassman, "tell her, cut it out I am get mad soon. She cries. Calls me a shit. Says Bassman, you got to marry me. I say, look, man marries a woman, she starts in on him, get a job, go to work, every day, make money, save money, all that shit I am not good at. So, I don't marry you, you are not so angry all the time. You marry me, you will be."

"Oh," said Du Pré.

"So," said Bassman, "she is the saloon, having a drink, while I am out here getting the stuff. That is the way it should be."

"Them poor people, the roadhouse," said Du Pré, "they are shitting pickles. Good thing Madelaine grabs them, the cops be all over you. Dope you got all the time, I be playing Deer Lodge Prison with you."

"God watch over me," said Bassman. "Now, I am through, packing my shit here. You want to give me the rest of the sermon, you do it while I am sucking on a beer."

"OK," said Du Pré.

"Shut up," said Bassman. "You are my cousin, they kill each other a lot. Read the papers. *I couldn't take, no more, his bullshit.*" Bassman got in his van. Du Pré got in front. He looked at the hole in the windshield."

"Insurance cover this?" said Du Pré.

Bassman started the engine.

"Insurance. They got this law, North Dakota, you can't get no insurance, you don't have driver's license," said Bassman.

Du Pré nodded.

"They got no manners there," said Bassman. "I play good, you know, do this gig, South Dakota, I am driving along home, cop pulls me over. I got this hole, the floor, drop the dope out on the highway. Makes my throat dry, I have beer, drop the bottle out, the highway. So I am a clean ver' law-abiding citizen. Cop, little sawed-off white prick, he say *you walk down that white line.* He don't like the way, me, Bassman, walk. He take me to jail. Tells me, blow in this tube. Me, I say you go blow, dead coyote, you."

Bassman drove on up the street.

"So," said Bassman, "things, they sort of fall apart after that."

Bassman parked by the Toussaint Saloon.

"So they take my driver's license," said Bassman, "and the rude fucker don't give it back."

Du Pré laughed.

"Insurance," said Bassman.

They went on in.

32

Bassman's burlap blonde was sitting at the bar talking to Madelaine and Bart and a girl Du Pré didn't know.

Bart's niece, Du Pré thought.

Sour-looking kid. Pissed-off-looking kid.

Du Pré and Bassman stood at the bar. Madelaine brought a ditch for Du Pré and a beer for Bassman.

Bart and the girl got off their stools and came over.

"My niece Julie," said Bart.

Julie found something fascinating and urgent on the floor six inches or so in front of her black-painted toenails. She tugged at a silver stud punched through her lower lip.

"This is Mr. Du Pré," said Bart, "and Bassman. Fine musicians."

Julie mumbled something.

"Kim," said Bassman to his burlap blonde, "you maybe take this shitbrain kid out, talk to her."

"Sure," said Kim, getting down. She grabbed Julie by the shoulder and shoved her out the side door before the girl knew she was moving.

"Kim got a couple of those," said Bassman, "nails in their heads and shit. She knows, talking to them."

"Ah . . . ," said Bart.

"Bart," said Madelaine, "it is all right. Come here. Talk to Madelaine. Drink your soda pop. You got about as much brains to deal with that little bitch as that stuffed moose head over there. You let me, Kim, handle this."

"OK," said Bart.

"Don't get smart," said Madelaine, "don't say to yourself, ah, me, Bart, me, I know what to do now. You don't never know."

"OK," said Bart.

Madelaine patted his hand.

"You make a good husband and father someday," said Madelaine.

"What are Kim's kids . . . doing?" said Bart. He was looking hard at Bassman.

Bassman sighed.

"Ver' disappointing," he said. "Boy, he got music in him, but Kim she terrify the little shit into doing good in school. He gets over being scared, starts to like school. He is at that University of Wisconsin, studying uranium. Bombs and shit."

"Physics?" said Bart.

"Yeah, that," said Bassman. "I thought physics was that shit you give horses, make them puke."

"Oh," said Bart.

"Girl, she is getting that nursing degree, so she can be a doctor," said Bassman.

"Pre-med?" said Bart.

Bassman shrugged.

Bart looked at Bassman.

"What the fuck is Kim doing with *you?*" said Bart.

"Shooting at me, some of the time. She like the music," said Bassman. "I got this huge dick, too."

"She tell you that?" said Madelaine.

"She ain't the only one," said Bassman.

"Bassman," said Madelaine, "you go on, play that good music, dodge them bullets, shit like that. You are so dumb, Kim about got to water you twice a month is all."

"She say that, too," said Bassman. "Now, you going to go on, the compliments, or maybe I can have another beer?"

"Oh, you bet," said Madelaine, fishing one out of the cooler.

"What is Kim doing with Julie?" said Bart.

Bassman sucked down his beer.

"Having a nice big joint," said Bassman.

"Jesus Christ!" said Bart, "my sister'll kill me! She sent Julie here to get her away from all that."

"Bart!" yelled Madelaine, "what I just tell you!"

"Oh," said Bart.

"*Sit down!*" said Madelaine.

Bart sat down and looked bewildered.

Madelaine patted his hand.

"You got to trust us," she said.

"My sister'll kill me," said Bart.

"*Non,*" said Madelaine, "we see she don't. You get smart, try to think on this, tell Julie you got, do this, do that, that kid blow up like a volcano, get in trouble. Then your sister she *will* kill you."

Bart looked beseechingly at Du Pré.

"They got this union, man," said Du Pré. "Don't fuck with them."

Bart shook his head.

"Why me?" he said.

"Builds character," said Madelaine.

"I don't want any more character," said Bart.

"Me, either," said Bassman, "but we get it anyway."

Susan Klein, the owner of the saloon, came in.

"Lo!" she said, smiling.

She looked around the little group.

"Parents and Teachers Association meeting?" she said.

Bart nodded. Then he looked up.

"How did you know?" he said.

"Well," said Susan, "I heard your niece was coming to stay with you for a while."

"So," said Bart, "so what?"

Susan patted Bart's hand.

"I'm a mother, kid," she said. "Now, don't you worry, everything's gonna be all right."

Bart nodded.

CHAPTER

8

"You want me to do *what*?" said Bart.

Madelaine looked at him with real pity before her eyes narrowed down to mean slits.

"Your sister, she tell you what happen, Julie?" said Madelaine.

"She was hanging around with the wrong people," said Bart.

"I been doing that all my life," said Madelaine. "They are more interesting than the right people."

Bart thought about that for a moment.

"Julie, she was a gymnast," said Madelaine, "damn good, too, made the Olympic team almost. Then she really starts turning into a woman. Tits, hips, those things. You know about those things."

"I read about them once," said Bart.

"So," said Madelaine, "she is, she thinks, too *fat* to be a gymnast."

"OK," said Bart.

"She wants to be a gymnast. Thing she does in her life better than anything else and better than almost anyone else does it," said Madelaine.

"OK," said Bart.

"But she is a woman now, so she can't be a gymnast anymore, she gets a little slower when she gets a little heavier," said Madelaine.

"OK," said Bart.

"All you are wanting to do you can't do, you get upset," said Madelaine.

"OK," said Bart.

"Made her special," said Madelaine.

"OK," said Bart.

"So get her the fucking airplane," said Madelaine.

"Her mother will kill me," said Bart.

"Not before I do," said Madelaine, "and I am closer. Your sister, she is in Portland."

Bart nodded.

"Don't cost much, the ultralights," said Madelaine.

Bart rubbed his eyes.

"It's dangerous," he said.

Madelaine grabbed Bart by the throat and she pulled his face down to hers.

"GRRRRRRR," she said pleasantly.

"OK," said Bart.

"Bozeman," said Madelaine. "They sell them there."

"No!" said Bart, "Bozeman is full of goddamned yuppies and general purpose assholes and I hate it and it's not fair."

"Missoula," said Madelaine.

"Bozeman it is," said Bart.

"Now," said Madelaine, "you get to be a really good uncle and take your niece to Bozeman, let her pick out her airplane."

"She really wants one?" said Bart.

Madelaine sighed.

"She does but she doesn't *know* that yet," said Madelaine.

"Oh," said Bart.

"I think he's getting it," said Kim. She put her cigarette out in the ashtray.

"Give up," said Bassman. "Just go get the fucking airplane. I am tired, listening to you squawk."

.

Du Pré stared off at the wall. It was a really nice wall.

"Go pick her up at school," said Madelaine. "Just say you have to take her to an appointment. Surprise her!"

"Women like surprises," said Kim, "long as they know about 'em in advance and it is the right sort of surprise."

"Du Pré . . ." said Bart.

"Nice wall," said Du Pré.

Bart went out and they heard his big SUV start and roll away.

"OOOOOKAAAY," said Kim. "Bassman and I must away to deepest North Dakota."

"Nice meeting you," said Du Pré.

"Don't give him no slack," said Madelaine, pushing a twelve-pack of beer across the counter. Bassman tucked it under his arm and he nodded.

"Two weeks we do the roadhouse again," said Du Pré.

"He'll be there," said Kim.

Bassman belched long and pleasurably.

"Time we get back," said Kim, "he'll be better."

Du Pré looked at Madelaine and then at Bassman and Kim as they went out. Bassman was dressed like a wino and Kim had on her leathers and high black boots.

"She is a redhead," said Madelaine. "Next time we see them she will be anyway."

Du Pré shook his head.

"Got ever'thing figured out," he said.

"Most," said Madelaine, "of the time."

"How you know about that Kim?" said Du Pré.

"Know what?" said Madelaine.

"She is not going, kill Bassman," said Du Pré.

"I talk to Kim, six months ago maybe. She is ver' smart. She want that Bassman dead, he would be dead. She is shooting at him, some twenty-five, she does not want him dead. She just wants him, pay attention."

"How come you don't shoot at me?" said Du Pré.

"Haven't had to yet," said Madelaine.

She went back to beading the little purse she was working on.

38

The bar telephone rang and Madelaine answered it, then handed it to Du Pré.

"Is this Gabriel Du Pré?" said a voice, a man's, very soft.

"That is me," said Du Pré.

"Ah. Good," said the voice. "I . . . represent a man who wishes to be anonymous. He understands that you have some journals buried by the Lewis and Clark Expedition, specifically ones written by William Clark."

Du Pré waited.

"My client will offer you ten million dollars for them," said the voice.

"Not for sale," said Du Pré.

"My client will be very disappointed," said the soft voice. "Do you want more money than that?"

"Not for sale," said Du Pré. "Goodbye." He hung up the telephone.

"Somebody wants the journals," said Du Pré. "Offer me ten million dollars."

Madelaine nodded.

"Think that you have them," she said.

Du Pré nodded.

The telephone rang and rang.

Du Pré went to it and he picked it up.

"Mr. Du Pré," said the soft voice, "my client means to have those journals."

"Not for sale," said Du Pré. "Don't call back again."

"You will hear from me," said the voice. The line went dead.

"Same guy," said Du Pré.

Madelaine nodded.

"What him say?" she said.

"Him, he say, *My client means to have those journals,*" said Du Pré.

"It is a threat," said Madelaine.

Du Pré shrugged.

Madelaine held a bead on her needle and she put the tip of the steel through the buckskin and she drew the bead into the pattern.

"Don't say any more?" said Madelaine.

Du Pré shook his head.

Madelaine nodded.

"Be careful," she said.

Du Pré looked at her.

"Him don't make threats," said Du Pré, "him just say, you will hear from me."

Madelaine nodded. She picked up another bead with the point of the needle.

"Not a threat," she said, "just don't seem right."

Du Pré looked at her.

"What?" he said.

Madelaine picked up the telephone from behind the bar and she set it on the scarred wood in front of Du Pré.

"Kids they were calling here, making dumb jokes," said Madelaine, "So Susan got one of them things, tells you where the call is from, the number."

Du Pré nodded.

Madelaine tapped on the little crystal display.

"Don't got a number there, Du Pré," she said.

"Shit," said Du Pré.

CHAPTER

9

Du Pré pushed the levers and the old one-lung donkey engine hacked and coughed and the cable tightened and the log began to rise up.

"OK OK OK," yelled Raymond, "don't you knock me off here!"

He was up on top of a jungle gym made of logs pegged together, with ropes here and there and an old cargo net draped off one side.

The ancient crane shuddered and clanked and squealed and creaked.

Du Pré pulled back on the levers, slowly, and the log began to swing over toward Raymond, who threw a light rope around the end and then he moved away.

He tugged gently and the log swung four or five feet.

"Down!" he yelled.

Du Pré pulled all the way back on two levers and he tugged a bit on a third and the log dropped into place.

Raymond moved to the other end. He put his shoulder against the log and he shoved and it dropped into the socket.

"Good!" said Raymond. He lifted a huge electric drill and he bored a hole clear through the log and the socket beams and then he set the drill down and he picked up a sledge and a long peg and he drove the peg home.

He carried the drill and the sledge down to the other end and he did the same thing there.

"Done!" he said.

Several of Madelaine's children looked up at the jungle gym with dubious expressions.

Raymond let down the drill by its cord and he looked carefully below and he dropped the sledge.

Du Pré pulled the cables up, the weight on the end swaying, and then he locked them and he shut off the engine.

It was suddenly quiet.

The air was filled with thick blue smoke from the old engine's exhaust.

"He is trying, kill us," said Alcide, looking up at the logs.

"So many, you little shits," said Du Pré, "maybe he is culling his herd here."

Pallas grinned at her grandfather.

"Lots of lawsuits maybe," she said.

"Who you going to sue?" said Du Pré. He put his arm around her.

"Everybody!" said Pallas.

"OK!" said Raymond. "I have to go, work now. You have a good time on that!"

"I don't see you again, Papa," said Alcide, "give my stuff to . . . Hercule."

"This morning," said Raymond, "you and Hercule beating the shit out of each other."

"Yeah," said Alcide, "he got a black eye and I feel bad. I am going to die now. It is the least I can do."

"All these thanks," said Du Pré, "I am going, have some lunch."

The kids scrambled up the jungle gym and shrieked with joy.

Du Pré got in his old cruiser. He looked across the street, at a little white SUV. There was a young woman at the wheel. She had a camera pointed at him.

Du Pré sighed and he started the engine and he drove down to the Toussaint Saloon.

The little white SUV followed.

Du Pré parked and he got out.

The SUV pulled up beside him.

The young woman opened the door and she stood up and she looked at him.

"Gabriel Du Pré," she said.

Du Pré nodded.

She marched toward him, hand out. They shook.

"Allison Ames," she said. "I am doing an article on the lost journals of the Lewis and Clark Expedition. Would you answer a few questions? I will be happy to buy lunch."

"Non," said Du Pré, "I buy my own lunch."

He tipped his hat to her and he walked away, shaking his head.

"I am staying until I get the story!" said the young woman.

Du Pré ignored her.

He went in to the cool dark main room of the Toussaint Saloon. Susan Klein was on her high stool behind the bar, knitting.

Du Pré mixed himself a drink and he came round and sat. He rolled a smoke.

The door opened and Allison Ames came in.

"Out!" said Susan Klein. "Right now! I told you you may not come in here again, or trespass on my property. I meant it. Go!"

"I'll sue!" said Allison Ames.

A shadow rose behind her.

"Miss," said Sheriff Benny Klein, "this here's a court order. You are not to come on this property again. I will arrest you if you do. Leave now."

Allison Ames retreated and Benny came in.

"Dear Lucky Customer," said Benny, "you may have won a million dollars."

"Benny," said Susan, "I thought you got the court order."

"Not yet," said Benny, "had to make do with this crap. Hi, Du Pré."

Du Pré laughed.

"What she do here?" he said.

"She came in this morning," said Susan, "and started asking questions. Then she offered me money if I would call you and ask the

43

questions she wanted answered. I got a little hot at that. She has no manners."

Du Pré sighed.

"I maybe send her to Benetsee," he said.

"Du Pré," said Susan, "the last time you played a joke on Benetsee, you ended up in jail in North Dakota. Remember?"

Du Pré nodded.

"OK," he said, "Pelon maybe."

"Poor Pelon, the apprentice sorcerer," said Susan Klein, "who was last seen starving himself to death on Box Butte. By the way, has anyone been up there to see if he's dead or anything?"

"Long climb," said Du Pré. "But I look over there each morning, there are no buzzards, I say, Pelon, him, he is holding up well."

Susan squinted at her knitting.

"Damn," she said, "dropped a stitch."

She fussed with the wool.

"These damn journalists," said Susan. "God, they are pushy. I guess as the Bicentennial of the Lewis and Clark Expedition gets closer they will get worse."

"Well," said Benny, "not much we can do about it."

Du Pré nodded.

"She is worse than most," said Susan. "I wonder who she writes for."

Du Pré laughed.

"Trust fund snot," he said. "She is waiting, sell it."

"Ah," said Susan. She picked up the pace of her needles.

"Maybe I tell her, Pelon is fasting, praying, and him, he is the one knows about the journals."

"Du Pré," said Susan, "quit. With Benetsee picking on Pelon you don't have to pile on."

Du Pré nodded.

"Me," he said, "we find those things and then there is all of that trouble. Government suing me. Bart he finds me a lawyer, but me, I don't know where those things are now, Benetsee has them."

"They figure you can get 'em from him," said Benny.

"They can go get them from him," said Du Pré.

Like those two fools, the Forest Service, come to give Benetsee a ticket for his sweat lodge fire. Benetsee show them fire. He show them how it can run, turn green and blue, dance in the trees and not burn them. Forest Service men, they look each other once, run, don't come back.

Du Pré finished his drink. He went to the john and then he came back and he clapped his old hat on his head and he went out.

Allison Ames and the little white SUV were still there. She took several pictures of Du Pré when he went to his old cruiser and he got in.

He looked at the dashboard.

There was an ordinary white envelope there.

Du Pré looked at it for a moment.

It wasn't sealed.

There was a thick wad of hundred-dollar bills there, and a single yellow stick-on note.

"You need to talk to us," it said.

Du Pré put the flap back inside the envelope.

He tossed it out the window and he backed out and he drove off.

The little white SUV followed.

CHAPTER
10

The ultralight aircraft zipped down the asphalt road and it lifted into the air very slowly, and Julie climbed at a very shallow angle until she was perhaps a hundred feet above the earth.

"Jesus," said Du Pré.

Bart nodded grimly.

"She had some lessons," he said, "and took off. You don't need any sort of license for them."

"Probably they don't live long enough to bother with," said Du Pré.

"I needed that," said Bart. "That friendly, supportive word. It is so good to have friends to help at times of stress."

"Sister going to kill you, huh?" said Du Pré.

"I won't die alone, you half-breed son of a bitch," said Bart.

Julie banked, very slowly, and she sailed out over the sagebrush.

"She is pret' good," said Du Pré.

"She should be," said Bart. "She has amazing strength and reflexes. She's a small woman, but graceful. Very graceful. I watched a couple of videos Angie sent me. She worked the horse and the parallel bars and most strikingly the free exercise."

Du Pré nodded.

Little tiny girls all horn and wire. Grows some tits and hips and she is past her prime.

Du Pré grimaced.

"What?" said Bart.

He shook his head.

"What?" said Bart.

"It is all the same crap," said Du Pré. "Gymnastics, those people, lifting weights, take drugs, die young. Race horses, bred for speed got weak legs. Me, I do not like people wanting to win some dumb contest so bad they make freaks of people, animals."

"Yeah," said Bart.

"I give up fiddling contests," said Du Pré.

"That'll show 'em," said Bart.

Du Pré sighed. He nodded.

"It is not the same, I guess," he said.

Julie came back toward them. She went overhead, the little engine snarling and screaming.

"Amazing," said Bart.

Julie made a long wide bank. She lined herself up with the highway and she began to descend. She got to two feet above the blacktop and she gently set the funny little machine down on the tiny wheels. She cut the engine and the ultralight slowed down and then she stopped it by putting out her feet and dragging her heels. She cut the engine altogether. She grinned, her teeth white and her face happy, encased in the helmet.

"Wow, wow!" she said. She undid the harness and she stood up.

A little puff of wind lifted one wing.

Bart helped her break down the little aircraft and they put it in the back of his big pickup. They hooked bungee cords here and there.

Du Pré got in the back of the crew cab and Bart and Julie got in front. Bart started the truck and he turned it around and they headed to Bart's place.

Bart pulled up to the machine shed. They got out and hauled the ultralight off the tailgate and carried it in and set it down next to a huge Caterpillar tractor.

"So we got a deal?" said Bart, looking at Julie.

Julie nodded.

"I don't have a lot of practice at this," said Bart.

"You're doing fine," said Julie. "Mom was on my case all the time and I got tired of it. You know, do your schoolwork. I didn't *want* to do schoolwork. I wanted to be practicing. Then there wasn't any point in practicing."

"Kid," said Bart, "old fart I know told me once that in life what you lose on the roller coaster, you make up for on the merry-go-round."

"Yeah," said Julie. "Can I have a smoke?"

"No!" yelled Bart. "God damn it! You're too young to smoke! It is bad for your health!"

Julie shrugged.

"I'm thirsty," she said.

They went up to Bart's house.

There was a thump on the door and Booger Tom came in, walking a little stiffly.

The old cowboy looked at Du Pré and Bart and Julie.

"Yer a sorry-lookin' bunch," he said. "What happened? You was all just a standin' around mindin' your own business and a coyote come outta nowhere and pissed on yer boots?"

Julie laughed and laughed and laughed.

Bart and Du Pré grinned at Booger Tom.

Julie got up from her stool.

"You want coffee, Mister Bodine?" she said.

"That would be nice, Missy," said Booger Tom. "These two sorry sons of bitches ain't been givin' you too much good advice, have they?"

"Yeah," said Julie. "Could ya just shoot 'em?"

"God damn, Missy!" said Booger Tom, "thought ya'd never ask! Been waitin' years fer a chance, maybe ta do somebody a real favor. I'll be right back!"

"Enough!" roared Bart.

"Tch-tch-tch," said Booger Tom. "Sensitive, ain't he?"

"I got to go," said Julie. "Thanks, Uncle Bart."

She went out the door with Booger Tom.

"Julie, she seems, be doing well," said Du Pré.

Bart nodded.

"I dunno about raising kids," said Bart. "Angie . . . maybe she and Julie just got in a wrangle and they couldn't figure out how to get out of it."

"She is sixteen," said Du Pré. "It is hard, that. She is the best at something, then she can't do it anymore."

"Dear Sis," said Bart, "I am trying to kill your daughter with very dangerous toys. My foreman is trying to kill your daughter with very dangerous horses. We should succeed soon. Love, your brother. I do need to write that letter. That kid, for chrissake, I oughta be grateful she doesn't want to race stock cars."

"You ask her?" said Du Pré.

"Please!" said Bart, "and for God's sake tell Madelaine to keep her trap shut."

"*Non,*" said Du Pré. "I got, me, all my own teeth, balls, I don't want lose them."

"Yeah," said Bart, "I forgot about that."

"So she is doing fine," said Du Pré.

"If anything happened to her I'd lose my mind," said Bart.

"She is a good kid," said Du Pré. "Tough kid. She is ver' tough."

"Well," said Bart, "I made a deal with her. She does well in school, she can try to kill herself in her spare time."

"Maybe she don't like school," said Du Pré.

"I got to do *something!*" said Bart.

"Yeah," said Du Pré, "thinking, that kind, get us into this war, Vietnam."

"What do I do?" said Bart. "Give up?"

Du Pré nodded.

"You will have to later anyway," he said. "I did, after that, things settle down, my daughters. They take care of *me.*"

"Oh," said Bart.

"I am trying, run their lives before," said Du Pré, "wonder I am not found, head down in a badger hole, some dead."

"Oh," said Bart.

"Anyway," said Du Pré, "don't talk, me, talk, Madelaine."

"She has more brains," said Bart.

Du Pré drank his coffee.

Julie shrieked out in the corral.

YAHOOOOOOOOOOOOOOO!

"I got this bad feeling," said Du Pré.

Bart looked up.

"This woman, Allison Ames," said Du Pré, "says she is a journalist. She follows me. The Lewis and Clark stuff. I am in the bar, I come out, there is this envelope, got a wad of hundreds in it. I get this phone call, the bar, saying, we want that Lewis and Clark stuff. I throw out the envelope, I say no on the telephone."

Bart nodded.

"Susan Klein she put that thing, the phone, gives the number that is calling you—" said Du Pré.

"Caller ID," said Bart.

"Yeah," said Du Pré, "but this call I get, it don't show the number."

Bart looked up, sharply.

"Why didn't you tell me this?" he said.

Du Pré shrugged.

Bart had his cell phone in his hand and he dialed.

CHAPTER

11

"I've seen the *fucking ballet*," said Julie. "I don't want to go."

"It's required," said Bart. "The teachers went to a lot of trouble to get the grants to take everybody down to Billings for the ballet. Now, quit whining. It would be rude to them if you didn't go."

"Christ," said Julie.

"Julie," said Bart, "please. I know you don't like school. They are trying very hard here. If you don't go, the other kids and their parents will think you're a rich snot, too good to go to Billings with them."

Julie sighed and she nodded.

"I am a rich snot," she said.

"Can't help that," said Bart, "but you do get things like ultralight aircraft out of it."

"OK OK OK," said Julie.

"Not bad," said Madelaine, reaching across the bar to pat Bart's hand. "You need, little practice laying on guilt, though."

Bart nodded. He rubbed his eyes.

"I have no talent for this," said Bart, looking miserable.

"Uncle Bart," said Julie, coming to him and hugging him, "if you are trying to make me feel sorry for you, you've succeeded."

"Getting better, him, huh?" said Madelaine, looking at Julie.

They both laughed.

Pallas and Berne and Alcide and Thierry were going down to Billings, too, to see the ballet. They were over in the corner playing a video poker machine for nickels.

Benny Klein came in. He looked at the kids in front of the gambling machines.

"Madelaine!" said Benny. "God damn it!"

"Kids!" said Madelaine, "away from those machines. The Baptists are here and they have guns!"

Benny looked down at his badge.

"Just a minute," said Pallas. "I about got a flush here."

"Criminals," said Benny.

"Got it!" yelled Pallas. "Big win!"

"For chrissakes," said Sheriff Benny Klein, "what if the liquor and gaming pricks come here. I am the sheriff and this place is owned by my wife!"

"They don't come here," said Madelaine. "You remember the last time that they come here?"

"Oh, yeah, that," said Benny.

"They come in, snoop around," said Madelaine, "go back out their car is on these four jackstands, all the tires are gone."

"Yeah," said Benny.

"It is the winter," said Madelaine.

"Yeah, I remember that," said Benny.

"They sit all night, the cold, in the car, no rooms are empty, it is late hunting season," said Madelaine.

"Yeah," said Benny. "I remember the call about the stolen tires."

"So this old liquor cop, he comes in here, says, please, we will go away and not come back for a long time. Just give us back our tires."

Benny nodded.

"Him, his two friends come in, have hamburgers, get warm, they go out, tires are back on the car, they go away," said Madelaine.

"Right," said Benny.

"So," said Madelaine, "what are you worried about?"

"Oh, just the fact that I took an oath to uphold the law," said Benny.

"You want to jump, ever' time those assholes in Helena want to run everyone's life?" said Madelaine.

Benny thought about that for a moment.

"This is Montana," said Benny, "and I am a Montanan. We obey any law we think is a good one and not in the way."

"Good," said Madelaine.

"Shit!" said Pallas. "I lost all my money!"

"Happens when you gamble," said Madelaine, "most of the time."

"OK," said Pallas. "We need to go."

Bart got up. He took the kids out the door.

"Could I have a hamburger?" said Benny.

"Sure," said Madelaine, "but maybe you better call Helena, see if those assholes made it illegal to eat meat."

"All right, all *right!*" said Benny, "I give up."

"I dunno," said Madelaine. "Maybe the law is, that tofu shit, all you can serve in bars in Montana, no smoking neither."

"Please," said Benny, "can I have my hamburger?"

"Sure," said Madelaine, "your wife, she owns this place."

Du Pré laughed silently and he turned back to his ditchwater highball.

"That Ames woman is still out there, sitting in the SUV," said Benny. "She's staying at the hotel in Cooper. Just staring at ya."

Du Pré shrugged.

"She's spreading money around, too," said Benny. "She knows about ol' Benetsee now."

"Good," said Du Pré.

"Yeah," said Benny. "Look, I can't do anything."

Du Pré shrugged.

"She will get tired, go away," he said.

"Probably," said Benny. "Pain in the ass while she's here."

Du Pré got up and he walked outside and he looked over at Allison Ames sitting in her little white SUV.

The envelope with the money in it was still in the parking lot, with tread marks on it.

Du Pré shook his head and he went back inside.

"I go out, few days ago," said Du Pré, "there is this envelope, got a bunch of hundreds in it, on my car seat. I toss it out the window. It is still there."

Benny sighed.

"Lost and found maybe?" said Du Pré. "Me, I do not want to go pick it up. She maybe put it in my car."

"OK," said Benny. He got up and he went to the door and Du Pré followed, and he pointed at the envelope in the drying mud. Benny went to it and he picked it up and he looked inside. He came back in.

"There's thousands of dollars here," he said. "Wonder no one picked it up."

Du Pré nodded.

Benny took out the soggy money and he counted it.

"Ten thousand dollars," said Benny.

Du Pré nodded.

"I get this phone call, man says he has someone wants the Lewis and Clark stuff," said Du Pré. "Then this envelope, has a note, says *You need to talk to us.*"

Benny nodded.

"This country," he said, "has too goddamned much money these days."

Madelaine came out of the kitchen with Benny's hamburger and fries. She set the platter down in front of him.

Benny squirted catsup on his burger and he laid the slab of red onion on top. He put on the other half of the bun.

He ate with pleasure.

"Me," said Du Pré, "I am going to see that Benetsee."

Madelaine nodded.

"You got wine?" she said.

Du Pré shook his head. Madelaine went in the back and she came out with a jug and she pushed it over the counter.

Du Pré went out to his cruiser. He put the wine in the trunk and he got in and he started the engine and he backed out and roared off to the west.

The little white SUV followed.

Du Pré drove up to the bench road and along it until he got to the rutted track that led to Benetsee's cabin. He bounced over the torn-up mud and he parked next to the big rock that lurked in the weeds hungry for oil pans.

There was no smoke coming from the chimney.

Du Pré walked around to the back and down the little hill to the sweat lodge, and he saw the doorflap up on top of the frame of willows.

No tracks on the ground.

He went back up the hill to the cabin.

The little white SUV was down on the county road. A camera lens was poked out of the window.

Du Pré looked at the porch. There was an old saddle blanket in front of the door, much caked with mud. Something white stuck out a little from under it.

Du Pré pulled the envelope out.

It had been there for a few days.

He didn't need to look in it.

CHAPTER

12

"Very interesting," said Foote's voice on the phone.

Du Pré waited, thinking about Bart's lawyer, in his English suits and shoes, in an office the size of a school here, with his feet on the desk.

"It bothers me," said Du Pré.

"Real menace," said Foote. "No threats. Just a shadow."

"Yah," said Du Pré.

"Well," said Foote, "Bart wants to have security out there *now*. What do you think?"

"Me, I do not know," said Du Pré. "They are leaving ten thousand dollars here, there, they don't care."

"Ummmhummm," said Foote.

"But nothing has been done that is threatening," said Du Pré.

"Like many rich people," said Foote, "Bart wants to be protected without seeing his protection."

Du Pré snorted.

"He wants you to make the decision," said Foote.

Du Pré sighed.

"Maybe we wait," he said. "Maybe this is a game, they go away."

"Possibly," said Foote, "and possibly they ratchet things up a bit."

"Yah," said Du Pré, "but there are no threats. Just money. That woman who is here, Allison Ames, she swears she has nothing to do with it. She say the envelope was left by a man who was driving some rental car. He came, parked with the engine running, put the envelope in the car, went away. He kept his face away."

"OK," said Foote, "and who the hell is Allison Ames?"

"Journalist," said Du Pré.

"For whom?" said Foote.

"I don't know," said Du Pré.

"For chrissake," said Foote, "then go and talk with her."

"She is a pest," said Du Pré.

"Talk to her anyway, if you don't mind," said Foote.

"I mind," said Du Pré.

"God damn it, Gabriel," said Foote, "please. Otherwise I have to send somebody all of the way out there . . . and that takes time."

"She will lie anyway," said Du Pré.

"Whatever," said Foote.

"All right," said Du Pré. He put the telephone back in its cradle.

Madelaine was sitting at the table in the kitchen, still in her robe. Her dark skin had a blush of red in it, and her black hair had crimson lights in it.

"Foote says I need to talk, that Ames woman," said Du Pré.

"Well," said Madelaine, "she will not be hard to find. She is probably out front right now."

Du Pré nodded. He poured himself some coffee and he went to the front door of the house and he opened it.

No little white SUV.

He shut the door.

"Not there," said Madelaine when he came back.

Du Pré shook his head.

"I got, go see about Benetsee again," said Du Pré. "That money, it worry me."

"You leave it there?" said Madelaine.

"Yes," said Du Pré. "I wonder who is doing this."

"Pret' good," said Madelaine. "Hard to hide, this country."

Du Pré went out to his cruiser and he got in and he started it. He drove out of town and he turned north to go up on the bench road.

He rolled a smoke.

It was warming up now.

The snow on the peaks of the Wolf Mountains blazed white in the morning sun.

Du Pré stopped at the track that led up to Benetsee's cabin. He looked carefully at the dirt.

His tire tracks going out the night before.

Nothing come in since.

He drove on up, and he parked in the same place he had the afternoon before.

The cabin was cold and dark.

The envelope was still there, under the saddle blanket.

Du Pré looked at the porch.

He squatted down.

He went to his left and he studied the ground, and then he went down through the grass and sagebrush to the road.

Clear tracks, one man, six feet or so, one-eighty, moccasins or some other smooth-soled shoe.

He had hesitated halfway up to the cabin, then he had gone on.

Parked a small car by the roadside.

Come in the night, to check the envelope and see if the old man was home.

But Benetsee was gone, maybe far away.

Maybe looking down from the butte.

"Some tooth fairy," said Du Pré, "leaving ten grand. Old man got no teeth anyway."

Du Pré went around to the back of the cabin.

No one had been on the back porch.

A black bear had been by, hoping for food, and had gone on.

The ground around the sweat lodge had seen coyotes and white-tailed deer.

The creek was beginning to rise with meltwater.

Du Pré went back up the little rise and around the cabin to his cruiser. He got in and he backed around and he drove back to Toussaint, and he saw the little white SUV, parked over in the lot across the road from the saloon.

The lot was also the Toussaint Airport. The windsock was dancing.

Allison Ames was doing exercises by her SUV. She stretched and bent and danced, holding her hands out like they had charley horses in them.

"Ty chee," said Du Pré.

He parked by her SUV and he got out.

"Mr. Du Pré!" said Allison Ames, "you've come to talk to me!"

"Who you write for?" said Du Pré.

"Freelance," said Ames. "This is going to be a hot piece. I can sell it if I can get it."

"Who you sell it to?" said Du Pré.

Ames shrugged.

"I've got a good agency," said Ames.

"So how do I know you write things?" said Du Pré.

"Ah," said Ames. She went to the back of the SUV and she got a big white envelope. She handed it to Du Pré.

"Copies of some of my work," she said. "You may have it."

Du Pré looked at her.

"What is it you want?" he said.

"The whole story on the Lewis and Clark stuff you found," she said.

Du Pré nodded.

"Long story," he said.

"I got a lot of time," said Ames.

"I think about it," said Du Pré. He drove back to Madelaine's.

She was out in the yard peering at the first green shoots of the lilies and tulips and irises she grew in the raised beds on each side of the porch.

"Only a couple more blizzards it is spring," said Madelaine.

"They are looking pret' good," said Du Pré.

"OK," said Madelaine. "What is that there?" She nodded at the envelope.

"Ames stuff," said Du Pré. "She give it to me."

They went in the house.

Madelaine cooked some breakfast, slabs of ham and scrambled eggs with chiles and cheddar cheese, hot sauce on the side. Thick slices of her good bread, chokecherry jam.

Du Pré looked at the articles.

"*New York Times Magazine*," he said.

"OK," said Madelaine, "so she writes like she said she does."

"She got some money," said Du Pré. "Those others they starve out pret' quick they don't get what they want."

Madelaine chewed ham.

The telephone rang.

Madelaine got up and she answered it.

She listened.

"You, Bart," she said, "you calm down. You are where?"

She listened.

"You do that," she said. "We be there soon."

Madelaine put the phone back.

"Julie disappeared," she said.

Du Pré slapped the table, hard.

CHAPTER

13

Bart fidgeted in the back seat. He chewed an unlit cigar and he kept looking out the window at the country rushing past.

Madelaine turned and she put her hand on his knee.

"Calm down, Bart," she said. "She is, sixteen-year-old kid. She is pissed off. At ever'thing."

"I thought I was doing it right," said Bart.

"Nobody can do anything right, you are sixteen," said Madelaine.

Bart nodded.

"Who is her boyfriend?" asked Madelaine.

"What?" said Bart, coming out of his shock for a moment.

Madelaine looked at him, eyes full of pity.

"Sixteen," said Madelaine, "they become horny little bastards. All them glands. Glands pumping overtime. Girls, they get boyfriends then."

"Oh," said Bart.

"OK," said Madelaine, "I try another way. Who your niece fucking?"

"Jesus," said Bart.

"Him dead, long time," said Madelaine, "so maybe you call your sister, ask, who is Julie's boyfriend?"

"I never thought of that," said Bart.

Bart pulled out his odd little shoehorn telephone and he dialed and he waited. He turned away and mumbled into the thing.

Madelaine snorted.

Du Pré laughed.

Bart shut the phone up.

"Conor Burrows," he said.

"Him missing?" said Madelaine.

"For two days," said Bart.

"Ah," said Madelaine.

Du Pré roared.

"Goddamnit, Gabriel," said Bart, "quit picking on me."

"Dumb shit!" said Madelaine and Du Pré.

They turned on to the Interstate and Du Pré slowed down to eighty-five.

"Where would they go?" said Bart.

"A motel," said Madelaine and Du Pré.

Bart sighed and he looked out the window.

"She disappear yesterday," said Madelaine, "evening, so . . . they are still fucking their brains out someplace. Probably didn't get all that far, find a motel."

Bart nodded.

"Smart kids," said Madelaine, "so, they will figure ever'body will think they are from the West Coast, they will go, West Coast."

Bart chewed a knuckle.

A highway exit sign appeared.

MILES CITY.

Du Pré slowed and he turned off and he stopped at the sign and he turned left and went over the Interstate and he followed the main route into town.

Motels.

Madelaine pointed at one.

Du Pré turned in to the parking lot. He slowed.

There was a Volvo with Oregon plates parked in front of Room 119.

Du Pré pulled in beside it.

Madelaine got out.

So did Bart and Du Pré. They hung back.

Madelaine banged on the door.

Silence.

She banged again.

A curtain moved, just a little.

The door opened a crack.

A young man, blond hair all awry, peered out of the gloom.

"Conor Burrows?" said Madelaine.

The kid nodded.

"Sorry, bother you in mid-hump," said Madelaine, "but you, that Julie, put on your clothes. You are scaring ever'body."

The kid nodded.

"Shit!" screamed Julie, inside.

Madelaine pushed the door open and she went on in.

There was some yelling.

"How," said Bart, "in the hell did she know?"

Du Pré laughed.

"Madelaine knows kids," he said. "So, while ever'body is chewing the rugs, she call her cousin here, say, go see maybe there is a car, Oregon plates, a motel."

"Oh," said Bart.

The yelling stopped.

Madelaine came back out.

She grinned.

"You call your sister maybe?" she said.

Bart got out his telephone.

Goddamned thing works from a satellite, Du Pré thought, works anywhere. I don't like, modern times.

Bart walked away.

Du Pré rolled a smoke and he lit it and by the time he was through Conor and Julie were coming out of the room with their bags. They both looked down at the gravel of the parking lot.

"What were you—," said Bart, his face red.

"Shut up," said Madelaine. "You two, go on home. I ride back with them."

"What?" said Bart.

Du Pré grabbed his shoulder and shoved him in the car before he got in deeper.

Bart muttered to himself for the first fifty miles.

Du Pré reached down under the seat and got his flask and he had some whiskey and he rolled another cigarette and when the two-lane highway stretched north unbroken to the horizon he got the old cruiser up to a hundred and ten and he kept it there.

"GAAAAAAAAAAAAGGGGHHHHH!" roared Bart.

Du Pré nodded.

"Fine," said Bart. "What do I do now? Give those little bastards a house to fuck in?"

"Be easier to sleep, yours," said Du Pré. "Not so much noise, there at night."

"They are *sixteen!*" said Bart.

"Yah," said Du Pré.

"I'm supposed to keep Julie out of trouble," said Bart.

"Oh," said Du Pré.

"I am out of my depth," said Bart.

Du Pré nodded.

They shot over the top of a hill and down the long grade to the watercourse at the bottom. The cruiser sank on its springs and then slowly rose.

They didn't speak until they got to Toussaint. Du Pré wheeled in to the lot beside the saloon, next to Bart's big green SUV.

Du Pré got out and he went in.

Susan Klein was on her stool knitting. A few of the regulars were sipping red beers.

"Find 'em?" said Susan.

Du Pré nodded.

"Good," said Susan. "UPS brought you a package."

Du Pré went to it, sitting on the table nearest the bar.

He peered at the label.

Shipped from New York. The shipper's name was illegible.

Du Pré lifted it. It was light. The box was about thirty inches by fourteen and a foot or so deep.

He took out his pocketknife and he slit the tape and he folded the flaps back.

Compressible packing in slabs, done in thin gray plastic bags.

A case. A violin case.

Du Pré frowned.

Bart came over.

"This you?" said Du Pré.

"Nope," said Bart.

Du Pré lifted out the case and he flipped the clasps and he opened it.

A violin sat there, gleaming. It seemed to be old but very well cared for. The bow sat beside it.

Du Pré lifted out the violin.

The bow. He tightened the horsehair.

Du Pré tuned the fiddle, plucking the strings while turning the pegs.

He drew the bow.

A huge, rich sound filled the room.

Du Pré looked under the case.

A note.

You need to talk to us.

CHAPTER

14

"Well, send it on," said Foote. "Nothing has been done that is at all illegal. No threats have been made. Which, of course, makes it all the more menacing."

"OK," said Du Pré, "it is a beautiful violin."

"Perhaps," said Foote, "we can find out who made it and perhaps we can find out who bought it."

"It is no secret, I am a fiddler," said Du Pré.

"The money did not attract you," said Foote, "so they are trying something else. These people are very, very good. I'll see if our people have any ideas."

"Yah," said Du Pré.

Half the fucking CIA works for Foote. Russians fall apart they got to find new jobs.

"Let me know if anything else happens," said Foote. "The money is being run through a lab now. Did you know that virtually all circulated hundred dollar bills have traces of cocaine on them?"

"OK," said Du Pré.

He put the telephone back on its cradle.

He went out to his car and he got in and he drove to the parking lot in Cooper, by the grocery store.

The UPS truck was there. Du Pré gave the package to the driver.

He went to the package liquor store and bought two gallons of bourbon, in big plastic jugs.

It was about two in the afternoon.

Du Pré drove back to Toussaint.

He passed his old house, where Raymond and Jacqueline lived now, and he saw many cars parked in the drive and on the road.

Du Pré stopped. There was a crowd around the jungle gym he and Raymond had built.

Du Pré got out and he walked around back of the house.

Julie and Conor were up on the jungle gym, doing tricks.

Julie swung by her hands, stood, then snapped down and up and she turned in midair and caught another crossbar.

Conor followed.

Then Julie swung through the jungle gym, very fast, using her hands and hips, sinuous as a snake. It was graceful and complete.

Conor danced over the top of the gym, tumbling off the end, and catching himself easily, before flipping off and landing softly on his feet.

Julie followed, and then the two of them bowed to the audience.

Small kids whistled and cheered. Three young girls ran up to Julie and they talked to her very earnestly. Julie nodded her head.

"Papa," said Jacqueline, "you going, learn how to do that?"

"*Non,*" said Du Pré, "break my neck."

Alcide and Thierry and Pallas and Berne were transfixed.

"Lots of expensive casts," said Du Pré. "Maybe Raymond and me, we should take this back down."

"*Non,*" said Pallas. "Granpa, you would not do that."

Conor and Julie went back up the jungle gym, easy as monkeys in trees. They were graceful, effortless, and easy in their bodies.

"Excuse me," said a voice behind Du Pré, "might I come in there? I need to have a word with my son."

Du Pré turned.

A man was standing there, carefully. He was just in the street, off the property.

"Sure," said Du Pré.

"Eamon Burrows," said the man, when he got near. He held out a blunt broad hand. His grip was firm. He was dressed in often-laundered casual clothing, and deck shoes. A light windbreaker that had seen a lot of wear. His square, pleasant face was deeply tanned, furrowed with wrinkles around the eyes. He spent a lot of time outside.

Him a sailor, thought Du Pré.

"Conor!" said Eamon Burrows, "a word, my man!"

Conor looked at his father, and he came down the long ladder on the jungle gym, easily and quickly.

Eamon Burrows put his arm around his son's shoulders and the two of them walked out to the street, and then they talked, but very quietly.

Good, Du Pré thought, him, he is not trying to humiliate the kid. Talk to him like he is a man.

Julie had come down, too, and she leaned against the jungle gym carelessly, while watching Conor and his father.

"Eh!" said Du Pré. "You come on, Julie, I take you to the saloon, we have a pop while you wait, eh?"

Julie came gratefully. She didn't want to stay, distracted, and act cheerful for the kids.

Du Pré opened the door of his cruiser for her and he got in and he went down the street to the Toussaint Saloon.

Madelaine was behind the bar, beading a little purse. She had on her reading glasses, half-lenses. She held a needle up to the light.

Du Pré went behind the bar. He got a Coke for Julie and a ditch for himself. They sat in front of Madelaine.

"Nice man that Mr. Burrows," said Madelaine.

"Yeah," said Julie.

"So," said Madelaine, "two of you, don't want to be apart, eh?"

"I love him," said Julie.

Madelaine nodded.

"So what you want to do?" she said.

Julie looked away.

"Get married," she said. "I think we can in Idaho."

Madelaine nodded.

"What then?" she said.

Julie drank her Coke.

"Ever'body want to help," said Madelaine, "which is maybe not help. Maybe you got too many people, helping you . . ."

"Like that bitch Angela, my mom," said Julie.

Madelaine was down off her stool and over the bar like that. She grabbed Julie by the shoulders.

"She is your *mother*," said Madelaine. "You don't talk about her that way. You got troubles with her, calling names just makes them worse."

Julie's face crumpled and she started to cry.

Du Pré went to the bathroom and he stayed in there awhile. When he came out, Julie was wiping her nose and laughing, while tears still shimmered in her eyes.

Du Pré went outside so he wasn't inside.

Eamon Burrows and Conor arrived. Eamon was driving a boxy old Volvo station wagon, much eaten by salt air.

"Mr. Du Pré," said Conor, "this is my father."

"We met," said Eamon. He nodded to Du Pré and Conor went ahead of him up the steps.

Thank you, Eamon mouthed as he passed. His eyes were twinkling.

Du Pré sighed. He finished his cigarette and he flicked the butt into the street. He went in.

Julie and Conor and Eamon and Madelaine were deep in conversation. Julie was still snuffling. Conor kept his hand on her shoulder and his face steady.

Eamon Burrows looked earnestly at Julie and Conor.

"This a fair deal?" he said.

Conor and Julie looked at each other. They nodded.

Eamon Burrows shook Madelaine's hand. He went outside, and Du Pré went, too.

Eamon clapped his hands together, twice.

"Beautiful here," he said.

Du Pré nodded. Way things are supposed to be.

"You aren't an eavesdropper," said Eamon Burrows. "Madelaine talked those two into finishing their school years—Conor has just two months to go until graduation—and then he can come here for the summer."

Du Pré nodded.

"Good kids," said Eamon Burrows. "Actually, if the little shit loves her that much, there isn't a lot anyone can do."

"Him got to get an education," said Du Pré.

"Yeah," said Eamon, "that. Well, I have a long drive. Conor is to leave the day after tomorrow. If you are in Portland, give me a call."

He handed Du Pré a business card.

Balducci Boatyard, it said, with Burrows's name and phone number on it.

"Please thank Madelaine again," said Eamon Burrows.

He went to his old Volvo and he drove away. The car might be mangy in the paint, but it ran damn well.

Du Pré sighed.

Where is that goddamned Benetsee?

CHAPTER

15

"Some things of interest," said Foote.

Du Pré sighed. He was standing at the pay phone in the Toussaint Saloon.

"The package was sent from Atlanta, phony address, phony name. Someone took it to a service center there, a terribly busy place. There are no fingerprints in the package and there were none on the violin, which had been carefully oiled and rubbed. Considering the care with which these people remain anonymous, not surprising. The violin is rare and valuable. A Torino, made in a workshop in Italy around 1790. Some of them are the equal of famous makers, and there are very few of them. This one disappeared in the Second World War and did not resurface until you received it."

"How much?" said Du Pré.

"Fifty thousand," said Foote. "Of course, if this had been bought through legitimate channels, there would be a provenance, a record of seller and buyer."

"So it was stolen," said Du Pré.

"Yup," said Foote. "Nineteen forty-three, it was the property of a French family, Jews, all deported to the death camps. Some of their artworks eventually appeared in the market, but the violin did not. We can make a number of speculations, but no more than that."

"So far," said Du Pré, "there is seventy thousand dollars sent here one way or another."

"A lot of money," said Foote.

"OK," said Du Pré.

"I checked with our security people," said Foote. "They are asking around, paying for information. There hasn't been any crime, so there are no grounds for the police to enter into this. I find it very worrying. But then it does seem that all they want is for you to talk to them, and entertain an offer for the Lewis and Clark material."

"I don't have it," said Du Pré. "Benetsee, him got it."

"True," said Foote, "but you are easier to find than Benetsee."

"OK," said Du Pré.

"These people may not in fact be dangerous," said Foote. "Merely very determined. Since the advent of computers, very little privacy remains here in America."

"Somebody is leaving envelopes, messages," said Du Pré.

"That," said Foote, "is easy to do. Now, I would think you can trap whoever that is."

"I think I maybe know," said Du Pré. "This Allison Ames woman. She says she is a journalist. Got some magazine clippings. She is here, says she will stay until she gets a story, about the Lewis and Clark stuff."

"Possible," said Foote. "Too, there could be someone local who would take money for dropping off a couple of envelopes."

"With ten thousand dollars in it," said Du Pré.

"You are there," said Foote. "We can send some people, but so far Bart resists. He hates feeling like he has to be guarded all the time. He once asked me how he could get rid of all his money. I said that was easy enough, but no one willing to kidnap him would believe that he had. So it would not help him."

Du Pré laughed.

"And then it would be difficult for him to help other people. So he cursed for a while and that was where we left it."

"OK," said Du Pré. "I just got a bad feeling about this."

"And I," said Foote. "Enough so I will be sending a couple of people. They may or may not contact you. In the field, they demand autonomy."

Du Pré said thank you and he hung up.

Madelaine was beading and Susan Klein was knitting behind the bar. They both stopped when Du Pré came over.

"How much, the violin?" said Madelaine.

"Fifty thousand," said Du Pré.

"Somebody," said Susan, "wants that Lewis and Clark stuff bad."

Du Pré nodded.

"But they are not doing anything illegal," he said.

"How are they getting the money here?" said Susan.

Du Pré shrugged.

"Pay somebody," he said, "pay them a lot. Say, you want to make more, keep your mouth shut. They are not doing anything bad, so they do. A lot of people here need money."

"Ever'body needs money," said Madelaine, "Bart, too, but most people here they are just making it by."

"Seems funny, though," said Susan, "how these people who want that Lewis and Clark stuff could *find* somebody here."

"Computer," said Du Pré. "That phone call, number didn't show on your ID machine. The call was made through several computers, so that this machine here don't get information. Foote said that."

"I am tired of computers," said Madelaine. "They are nosing into everything so they can sell more stuff."

Susan nodded.

"Modern times," she said.

"Nose up everybody's butt," said Madelaine.

Du Pré sighed.

"These, ver' smart people," he said. "They are doing nothing against the law, maybe sometime they do but not now."

"They could do something," said Susan. "I mean, there was a lot of panic when little Julie disappeared."

"She ain't so little," said Madelaine.

"Kids," said Susan, her voice full of her own.

The door opened and old Booger Tom came in, walking a little stiffly. He limped over to the bar.

"Howdy, stranger," said Susan. "What brings you to town?"

"My boss sent me," said Booger Tom, looking disgusted. "I been given a damn nursemaid's job."

Madelaine laughed.

"Picking Julie up," said Susan. "My, how you've fallen."

"When I was—" said Booger Tom.

"—A kid I walked ten miles to school and back, it was uphill both ways, and when I got there I had to chop wood for the stove. All I had to eat was a raw turnip I had to peel myself . . . ," said Susan Klein.

"You went, that school, too," said Madelaine.

"We all did," said Susan.

"Could I have a red beer," said Booger Tom. "Being insulted is damned thirsty work."

Madelaine made him one, with extra tomato juice.

There was a roar outside, the school bus pulled into town, and in a moment the shrieks of kids out of the slam for the day.

Booger Tom turned around when Julie came through the door. She was laughing. She carried her knapsack in one hand and her coat in the other.

When she caught the bus in the morning there was frost, and by the time she returned it was warm.

Julie came over, and she stood behind Booger Tom.

"Is . . . this . . . my . . . chauffeur?" she said sweetly.

Booger Tom nodded.

"My peckerwood's uniform is at the dry cleaner's," he said, "along with my patience."

"Could I have a Coke?" said Julie.

Booger Tom turned just enough so he could see her out of the corner of one eye.

"You talking to me?" he said.

"No," said Julie, smiling. "I know better than to think you are a waiter. I want to try and ride that roan again."

"He's wrangy as hell," said Booger Tom, "too much horse fer ya."

Susan Klein pushed a Coke over the counter to Julie. She climbed up on the stool next to Booger Tom.

"Awwwww," said Julie, smiling at the old monster. "C'mon. I can kill myself and then you won't have to drive me around."

"You got a driver's license?" said Booger Tom.

"Nope," said Julie.

"You know how to drive?" said Booger Tom.

"Yup," said Julie.

"In Montana," said Booger Tom, "about more people don't got license than do."

"I have to take driver's education," said Julie.

"Well," said Booger Tom, "that's *something*."

"But right now I want to ride the roan," said Julie.

"Too much horse," said Booger Tom.

"Awwwwwwwwwwww," said Julie and Madelaine and Susan.

Du Pré snorted.

Julie and Booger Tom finished their drinks and they went out, still arguing about the roan horse.

"Poor old fart," said Du Pré.

"Bullshit," said Madelaine. "He loves it."

CHAPTER

16

Du Pré drove out toward Benetsee's cabin. He was going up the bench road when he saw the little white SUV turn ahead.

Du Pré slowed and stopped.

Allison Ames drove up, and she rolled down her window.

"He isn't there," she said.

Du Pré nodded.

"You want to talk about the Lewis and Clark stuff?" said Ames.

Du Pré shook his head.

Ames nodded.

"I'll be here, Mr. Du Pré," she said, "spring, summer, winter, and fall, and the year after that, too. I'm staying here until I get the story."

"No story," said Du Pré. "There is not one."

Ames looked at him.

"Big story," she said. "And you have people very interested in that material."

"You are the one leaving the envelopes," said Du Pré.

"Nope," said Ames. "I saw the guy put the one in your car. Lied before, pissed off, you know, he was in a hooded sweatshirt. Looked like a rental car, just tooled up to yours, opened the door, tossed in something, and was gone."

Du Pré nodded.

"I thought about following him," said Ames. "Would have if I had known what was in it."

Du Pré sighed.

"Wouldn't matter," he said, putting the cruiser in drive.

Obnoxious woman, Du Pré thought, very.

Benetsee's cabin was cold and dark, and when Du Pré walked around the land there were signs of animals and birds, but no people had been here for a while.

Du Pré walked back up to the cruiser and he backed out and he turned around and drove down to the county road.

He was about to pull out of the track when he saw a man standing by a big Suburban. The man was off on a snowplow turnaround, and he was looking through some large binoculars at the mountains behind the cabin.

Du Pré pulled in beside him.

The man kept his eyes on the country.

"Gabriel Du Pré," said the man, "good afternoon. I am Paul Beck. Foote asked me to come."

Beck put down the binoculars and he turned to Du Pré.

Du Pré nodded.

"You want a drink?" said Du Pré. He shut off the car and he got out, his flask in his hand.

Beck shook his head.

"Not just now," he said. "Now, Foote told me the very little that he knew, and he did feel some urgency in finding out just who it is who is playing such games with you. Interesting. Very interesting. These people are far too smart to make any threats. They let you worry. And, of course, smart people are a good deal more dangerous than stupid ones."

Du Pré laughed.

Beck pulled a thermos from his big Suburban and he poured some dark coffee into an insulated traveling cup. He sipped it.

"Bighorn sheep," said Beck, "down pretty low."

Du Pré nodded.

"Early in the spring, at least there is no snow down here," he said.

"So," said Beck, "what shall we do? I will want to attach some stuff to the telephones you get your calls on, for starters. I expect they won't tell us shit, but you never know."

Du Pré nodded.

"I've arranged to rent the Reece place," said Beck. "Fascelli owns it, through a couple of other companies. I'm a writer. Since I have three books published, it is plausible."

Du Pré looked at Beck.

"Spy novels, yes?" said Du Pré.

Beck's eyes twinkled, and then they became very sad.

He shook his head.

"Butterflies," he said. "I am an amateur lepidopterist. I've written the books, not about the butterflies so much as pursuing and collecting them. There's a very small market."

A small light began to flash in the Suburban, and then a soft whistle pulsed.

"Excuse me," said Beck. He went to the big SUV and he opened the door and he got one of the odd shoehorn telephones.

Du Pré turned away.

He looked up at the butte behind Benetsee's house. The golden eagles who lived higher up the mountains were floating just above it, hanging in the air.

"Du Pré," said Beck. He held out the telephone.

Du Pré put it to his ear.

"Gabriel," said Foote, "I see Beck has contrived to meet you."

"Yah," said Du Pré, "butterflies, he writes about."

"Yes," said Foote. "After retiring from his . . . former work . . . I would think butterflies a good subject for the rest of one's life."

"Oh," said Du Pré.

"Something further from the lab," said Foote. "It seems that the violin was packaged somewhere in Texas. There were pollen grains in the thing, and somehow it can be determined from those where a box was sealed."

"Oh," said Du Pré, "Texas."

"Right," said Foote. "I am well aware of your opinion of Texans. Beck is a Texan."

"I don't shoot him," said Du Pré.

"Thanks," said Foote. "How is Bart?"

"Julie runs him easy," said Du Pré. "She is teaching gymnastics."

"Good," said Foote. "I am glad you met Beck. We shall talk soon."

Du Pré shut up the weird telephone.

Beck tucked it back in his truck.

"So," said Beck, "other than the phone calls, the two envelopes of money, and the violin, there has not been anything else?"

Du Pré shook his head.

"There is this journalist, Allison Ames. She swears she will stay here until she gets her story," he said.

"She is in fact a well-regarded journalist. A damned fool like most of them, but she does fair work," said Beck.

Du Pré nodded.

"The old man who lives up there," said Beck, "he sounds quite wonderful. I would very much like to meet him."

"You are lucky you don't," said Du Pré. "Old son of a bitch drive people crazy, his damn riddles."

Beck laughed.

"Ah, yes," he said, "a saint."

Du Pré looked at him.

"I misspoke," said Beck. "A prophet. They are not always a pleasure to be around."

"No shit," said Du Pré. "Now, what you think about this? These people, the money, the violin?"

Beck looked off.

"Speculation," he said, "is all I have, and it is only that. The trouble with this sort of thing is how easily one becomes fond of a theory, and then forgets to weigh evidence carefully . . . but. Someone with a good deal of money wants those artifacts. They are not willing, certainly, to reveal themselves. Since there is a pending case in the matter, I would think that what they want is simple possession, without revealing who they are. . . . This suggests someone with a great deal of money and new money at that. For only recently have they made so much money that they may buy anything that they want. It is quite immature. They want to own something singular. Something *rare*. They most likely already have all of the gewgaws, and they are unsatisfying. They seem to understand simple trade-craft. There is no direct connection to them. If we find their agents, we will find that enough money has been paid them to quiet their misgivings, and, it is important to remember, so far they have done nothing illegal. . . . The menace is in how easily they found you, delivered messages, found Benetsee, delivered money, and tried to bribe you with the rare violin . . ."

Du Pré nodded.

"They aren't terribly patient," said Beck. "Refusals bring more offers, and quickly."

Du Pré nodded.

"I doubt," said Beck, "that they are themselves dangerous, but I fear in their obsession they may hire people who are very dangerous indeed."

Du Pré looked at him.

"I think," said Beck, "that right now things are not dangerous at all, but that they may become so, as they get no results."

Du Pré nodded.

"They are capable of some clever ploys," said Beck, "using random routes and blind stops for the telephone calls, couriers who no doubt haven't a clue what they are carrying, but since it isn't illegal it doesn't seem to matter . . . Computer nerds, I should think."

Du Pré nodded.

"It is so new, there is so much money in it," said Beck.

Du Pré looked at him.

"We have some ideas," said Beck.

CHAPTER

17

There were two new sets of bars and a gymnast's horse set up beyond the jungle gym. Neat blue nylon covers for the equipment were folded and piled fifteen or so feet away.

Alcide was struggling to swing himself gracefully around the upright handles on the top of the horse, but he kept falling off.

His cheering section gave him a round of raspberries.

Du Pré looked at the jungle gym. It had held up well and the wooden pegs were tight. He and Raymond had poured concrete footings to disperse the weight of the giant assemblage of logs.

Some of the handholds were already polished by hands.

"Pret' good," said Jacqueline, standing with her fists on her hips. She looked at those of her brood trying to imitate Julie's grace.

"Maybe they are killed off some," said Du Pré.

"Papa," said Jacqueline, "you are full of shit."

Du Pré laughed.

Julie was standing next to the low bars, patiently guiding Berne though the exercises.

Du Pré walked away and he drove down to the saloon and he

went in. Madelaine was behind the bar, setting cheeseburgers in front of ranchers.

"Hungry, Du Pré?" she said.

Du Pré nodded. He went behind the bar and he drew a beer.

A rancher looked at Du Pré and nodded and went back to chewing.

Du Pré rolled a smoke and by the time he stubbed it out a rare cheeseburger and fries and coleslaw were in front of him. Madelaine went down the bar filling glasses and taking orders, and then she was gone into the kitchen again.

The door opened and Bassman came in with Kim not far behind.

She had red hair now, dark red.

The black leathers were gone. She was wearing jeans and boots and a flowered shirt.

They slid up on stools next to Du Pré, one on each side.

"'Lo, Kim," said Du Pré. "You are still with this guy."

"No good in it," said Kim, "but I love the music, so what can I do?"

"You are not talking?" said Du Pré to Bassman.

"I not talking, her," said Bassman. "On the way here, she say, you, Bassman, maybe you get a job, huh?"

"No!" said Du Pré.

"Bullshit," said Kim. "What I said was if he treated the music more like a job perhaps he could reach more people."

"She said *job*," said Bassman.

"Have a drink," said Du Pré. "Me, I do not want to have to give you CPR for shock."

Madelaine came. She ignored Bassman and she reached across the bartop to take both of Kim's hands and they chattered for a few moments. Then Madelaine made a stiff ditch and she plunked it down in front of Bassman.

"Poor baby," she said, sailing away.

Bassman sucked morosely on his ditch.

"You be OK," said Du Pré. "Play tonight here yes?"

Bassman nodded.

He looked past Du Pré at Kim.

"You, Du Pré," he said, "you keep that woman away from me."

"Wimp," said Kim.

Madelaine sailed back with a cheeseburger for Kim.

"Hey!" said Bassman. "What about me?"

Madelaine looked at him.

"No hope," she said, moving on.

Bassman nodded. He finished his ditch and he went off out the side door toward his van and his weed.

Du Pré laughed.

Kim ate.

Madelaine came back. She pointed at Bassman's stool.

"Him sulking?" she said.

Du Pré nodded.

"I hurt his feelings," said Kim. "I said *job* to him."

"That'd do it," said Madelaine, "but maybe you go tell the dumb shit he will have a burger in three minutes or so."

"I go," said Du Pré.

He went after Bassman and found him sitting in his van sucking on a huge spliff.

"Your cheeseburger is ready," said Du Pré.

Bassman cut the end off the joint with a small pair of scissors and he followed Du Pré back inside.

"Job," he said, biting into his cheeseburger.

"Real work of art, ain't he?" said Kim.

The bar phone began to ring and ring and ring and finally Du Pré went to answer it.

"Gabriel Du Pré?" said a voice which sounded like it was under water.

"Yah," said Du Pré.

"Like the violin?" said the voice.

Du Pré waited.

"You need to talk with us," said the voice. "Really, the gifts are just that. We mean no harm."

"Non," said Du Pré, hanging up.

He went back to the bar and then he turned and he made for the front door.

His cruiser was parked down at the end of the long walkway that stretched clear across the front of the saloon.

He went to it.

Nothing.

A red Jeep pulled off the street and it bounced over some potholes and the driver stopped and looked and then he went to the edge of the barrow pit and parked. He got out.

Du Pré looked at him. College student, probably. There was a rack for a kayak on top of the Jeep. He was perhaps twenty, blond and tanned, wearing expensive outdoor clothing and low hiking boots. The young man fished a package out of the back of the Jeep and he walked into the bar.

Du Pré waited.

The young man came out again, and he walked down the long porch to Du Pré. He set the box down on the boards.

"Gabriel Du Pré?" he said. "That's for you."

Du Pré looked at him.

He took three steps and he grabbed the kid by the throat.

"Who . . . are . . . you?" he said.

"Hey!" said the kid. "I just brought the stuff to you. I was paid to do it. Jesus, man, let go!"

"Who paid you?" said Du Pré.

He let the kid go.

"I got a telephone call," said the kid, "offering me five hundred bucks to deliver a box to you. That's all. It's just books, for God's sake . . ."

"Who call you?" said Du Pré.

"Didn't say," said the kid. "I was worried about it being dope or something, but when I went to pick it up, it was just books. The box was open. The money was at my apartment in Missoula by the time I got back."

Du Pré nodded. He fished out his wallet and flashed his brand inspector's badge at the kid.

"You wait," he said. "You leave you are arrested before you go two miles." He went inside and he fished out a card and dialed a number.

The phone rang six times.

"Beck."

"I got this box brought here by this kid," said Du Pré. "He says he don't know who paid him."

"I'll be there— Where is there by the way?" said Beck.

"Toussaint Saloon," said Du Pré.

"Fifteen minutes," said Beck.

Du Pré went to the kid. He looked at him.

"What?" said the kid. "What's illegal about bringing you a box of books, man?"

Du Pré just looked at him.

He went to the box.

Books. Old books, some in the cheap buckram bindings libraries put on books worn out from use.

Du Pré looked at the titles.

Music.

Métis music.

Collections, and then some oral histories taken by Jesuit priests from the voyageurs.

Old books.

Old books that Du Pré would like to read.

To go with the old violin he would like to play.

CHAPTER
18

"We can look in the guts of the little bastard's computer," said Beck, "but it won't tell us anything."

They watched the red Jeep scoot out of town.

Du Pré looked at him.

"We'll look anyway," said Beck. "And the books. I need to list them and send them in. I doubt that will tell us much, either."

"Stolen from libraries?" said Du Pré.

"Nope," said Beck. "Whoever this is, they aren't doing anything criminal, yet anyway."

Du Pré shook his head.

"Feel like I got my own, spy satellite," he said.

"There is almost no privacy left," said Beck. "Information is money, and money finds a way."

They walked back into the saloon.

Bassman was sucking on a ditch, ignoring Kim, who was talking to Madelaine. They were laughing.

"Thanks," said Du Pré. He set the box of books on a table and Beck opened one and he tapped in some information on his laptop.

Du Pré slid back up on his stool and Madelaine got him a ditch.

"You are feeling better, Bassman?" said Du Pré.

"Some," said Bassman, "but it will not last."

Du Pré nodded.

"She is still talking mean to you?" said Du Pré.

Bassman nodded and addressed his ditch.

"I am going, Benetsee's," said Du Pré to Madelaine.

She nodded at him.

Du Pré walked over to Beck.

"I be back soon," he said.

Beck nodded.

"If you are going to see the shaman," he said, "I would like to come. This is the last one . . ." He tapped a few more times on the keyboard and then he waited a moment and he shut the little computer off.

"Let's take my rig," said Beck.

They got in. Beck plugged a jack from his dashboard into the little laptop and he pressed a button and he waited until a red light came on and he unplugged the jack and he started the engine.

He drove swiftly out of town and up to the bench road and along it toward Benetsee's. He turned off on the rutted track that led to the old man's cabin.

It was still cold and dark, but Du Pré found coals in the pit at the sweat lodge.

"He was here?" said Beck.

Du Pré looked around. He shook his head.

"Pelon," he said, "the young man who studies with Benetsee. Last night, middle of the night."

"Where does the old bastard go?" said Beck.

Du Pré shrugged.

". . . *above, winged, the earth itself* . . . ," said Beck.

Du Pré looked at him.

"A poem," said Beck. "There are people who feel that we were more human and a good deal happier before we started screwing around with crops and metals."

Du Pré laughed, and after a time so did Beck.

Some crows flew up on the mountainside.

"There?" said Beck.

"Maybe," said Du Pré. "Maybe a coyote."

Beck nodded. He yawned.

"Music tonight," he said. "That will be good. You should make some more recordings."

Du Pré shrugged.

"Or not," said Beck.

They got back in his big Suburban and Beck turned around and went down the track. He drove well, and fast.

Bassman, Kim, and Julie were carrying equipment inside. It was almost done. Du Pré and Bassman set up the sound system and they tested the microphones a couple of times.

"I am tired," said Du Pré. "I will go, sleep a while."

"OK," said Madelaine, "I call you seven-thirty maybe."

Du Pré drove to her house. He crawled into bed and he was asleep.

It took three rings on the telephone to bring him awake and he lifted the receiver just before the tape machine would have kicked in.

"Coffee," said Madelaine. "You sound dead."

"Yah," Du Pré grunted. He padded to the kitchen and he made some double-roast, very strong, and he showered and put on his Red River shirt and sash and doeskin pants and high moccasins. He drank the rest of the pot of coffee but still felt half asleep.

The bar was filling up and Du Pré said hello to his neighbors. About eight o'clock people who didn't live nearby came, and they sat at the back tables, some of them were dressed very expensively.

"You are famous some," said Madelaine. "You won't play in the cities so they come here, hear that Du Pré. Saves you, the driving, maybe getting busted, the whiskey."

Du Pré laughed and she slid a ditchwater highball across to him.

He drank it.

Allison Ames had a good seat right in front.

Bassman was outside, toking up. He came in fifteen minutes before they were to begin with Père Godin, who had driven from Turtle Mountain in his rusty old Oldsmobile.

The three musicians tuned up in less than a minute.

Du Pré started with *Baptiste's Lament.*

Beck was standing against the wall in the back, a drink in his hand, all through the first set.

Allison Ames had a small tape recorder on the table in front of her.

Du Pré finished his last song and he went to Allison Ames and he picked up the tape recorder and he popped it open and he took out the tape.

"Wasn't on," she said.

"Then why you have it on the table?" said Du Pré. "Playing games."

She shrugged.

"You need to talk with me," she said.

"*Non*," said Du Pré.

"It is a big story," she said.

Du Pré shrugged.

"Big story," said Ames.

Du Pré saw Bassman and Kim and Julie going out the side door. Bart wasn't in the saloon yet. He would probably come later.

Du Pré laughed.

Madelaine was moving fast, pulling drinks and sending orders to the kitchen. People laughed and touched glasses, and each other. The crowd was very happy.

Du Pré sucked on his ditch.

Père Godin was charming a woman at the end of the bar. Du Pré stretched. He felt a little stiff still from the sleep. Kim came back in, and she went into the women's john. Madelaine filled pitchers of beer.

Du Pré went behind the bar and he made himself another drink.

Kim came out of the bathroom and she made her way around the tables to the bar. She stood in front of Du Pré.

"Good music!" she grinned.

Madelaine rushed by, nodding.

"Yah," said Du Pré, "it is that."

"Julie is talking a mile a minute with Bassman," said Kim, "about playing the bass."

Du Pré laughed.

Madelaine stuck a drink down in front of Kim. She picked it up and sipped it.

"She's a good kid," said Kim.

Du Pré nodded. They chatted for a while.

Père Godin came to Du Pré and he nodded toward the stage.

"Yah," said Du Pré, "it is time."

He made his way there.

Damn Bassman show up when his spliff is gone, Du Pré thought.

They started to play without him.

One song. Two songs. Three.

Kim gestured, she would go and roust him.

She went out the side door.

Du Pré played a jig and Père Godin played it back.

The side door opened.

Kim's face was wild and full of horror.

Du Pré set down his violin and he started to run.

Beck was through the side door first.

CHAPTER

19

They watched the LifeFlight helicopter rise up and head south. As soon as the pilot got enough altitude he kicked in the jet engines and the lights moved faster and faster and in a moment the horizon swallowed them.

I get there, Bassman is bleeding, his head smashed, Du Pré thought, Julie she is choking, they hit her in the face with pepper spray. But Kim comes then and they go, out of the parking lot like jackrabbits. We will go after them but our tires are cut. Pret' good. I am playing everybody is here, inside.

"Now," said Beck, "it is a much different game."

Du Pré nodded.

"Benny, he goes like hell, calls for help but it is too late," said Du Pré. "They got the three roads to go on, there is some traffic, no place to put a roadblock that is good."

"Daylight would have helped," said Beck.

"Don't make any sense," said Du Pré. "Why they club Bassman? They are kidnapping Julie? What for?"

"No," said Beck, "it doesn't make any sense. I doubt your admirer has anything to do with this. Not the right style."

Du Pré nodded.

He turned. Allison Ames was standing close, trying to hear.

"Got your good story," said Du Pré. He turned back to Beck.

"I'm going to see if I can flush our friends out with this sorry bullshit," said Beck. "I expect that they will not like it one bit."

Du Pré nodded.

"You know," said Beck, "it could be a casual word. I mean if this fool who is playing games with us idly mentioned a large sum of money, the wrong ears could have heard it."

Du Pré nodded.

"Bassman probably won't recall much past a half hour before he got clubbed," said Beck. "Let's try Julie again."

They went back to the saloon and into the kitchen. Julie was sitting on a stool, a wet towel pressed to her face. She took it away. Her skin was an angry red and her eyes slits.

Beck cleared his throat.

"How you doin'?" he said.

Madelaine and Susan Klein were finishing the cleanup.

"OK," said Julie, weakly.

"You went to the van . . ." said Beck.

"Yeah," said Julie. "It was parked so there was . . . so the sliding door was on the far side, away from the bar. Bassman was just behind me. I stepped around the back of the van and got sprayed with that shit. It hurt and I couldn't breathe very well. I heard Bassman get hit."

Beck nodded.

"I was choking and rubbing my eyes," said Julie. "I tried to scream but my throat closed."

"You heard a car engine," said Beck.

Julie nodded.

"They drove off," she said. "No squealing tires or anything. Just drove off."

"They grabbed you?" said Beck.

Julie nodded.

"They dragged me . . . a little ways and then dropped me."

Beck waited.

"OK," he said.

"I'm sorry," said Julie. "I hurt so much I didn't pay attention."

Beck patted her on the shoulder.

He nodded to Du Pré and he headed out to the front room of the saloon. Du Pré followed.

Beck took a flashlight from his pocket and he went out the side door and across the now empty parking lot to Bassman's van. He stopped about ten feet from it.

Du Pré followed and he held out his hand for the flashlight. He played it back and forth slowly and he moved forward.

"Too many feet," said Beck.

Du Pré nodded.

"Julie was . . . where?" said Beck. Du Pré pointed to a place twenty or so feet from the front of the van. They went toward it very slowly.

"You're the tracker," said Beck. "I am going to go try and track down the little shit who has been playing the games with us."

He backed away ten feet before turning and heading for his big Chevy Suburban.

Du Pré sat on his heels and he played the light over the ground holding the flashlight low. Clods and stones cast long shadows.

Fifty people are here stomping around, the medical people, me, the cops.

"Might's well try an' figger out the Bible," said Booger Tom, from the shadows.

Du Pré laughed and he stood up.

"Where is Bart?" he said.

"I locked him in that paint shed over by the power pole," said Booger Tom. "I thought he was about to a-tack the whiskey."

Du Pré nodded.

My poor friend thinks this is all his fault, so he gets mad at himself.

"We let him out now maybe," said Du Pré.

Booger Tom led Du Pré to the paint shed. He took a pin out of the hasp and he slid the door open and Bart stepped out. His face was red and puffy. He'd been crying.

He looked at Du Pré and Booger Tom.

"Thanks," he said.

"Julie is in there," said Du Pré. "You maybe go talk with her."

Bart nodded and he walked away.

"He'll be all right now," said Booger Tom. "This ain't something poor ol' Bart kin take good."

"What you think, my friend?" said Du Pré.

"Too old ta think," said Booger Tom. "Makes my ears droop."

"Pret' bad stuff," said Du Pré.

"Over them damn journals," said Booger Tom. "It was me, I'd burn the damn things. Nothin' but trouble."

Du Pré laughed.

"When Bart says his little niece is a-comin'," said Booger Tom, "I says, well, she'll rip his nuts off easy enough."

Du Pré slowly shook his head.

"Come mornin'," said Booger Tom, "I believe I will look around fer one of them little objects."

Du Pré nodded.

"That little bitch clubbed pore ol' Bassman with a damn tire iron, sure as shit," said Booger Tom, "and she puts it back where she got it and she sprays herself with that pepper crap and throws the can, I think."

Du Pré nodded.

"Don't need a damn roadblock," said Booger Tom.

"Why you think this?" said Du Pré.

"Same goddamned reasons you do," said Booger Tom. "They got plumb away 'cause they was never here in the first place."

"Maybe," said Du Pré.

"I 'spect the tire iron or whatver she spotted in the back of a pickup and she put it back and then sprayed herself," said Booger Tom. "But she had to get rid of the dingus, now, didn't she?"

Du Pré shrugged.

"Bassman was slugged in the back of the head," said Booger Tom.

Du Pré nodded.

"She run off once already," said Booger Tom.

Du Pré nodded.

He played the light around more. He bent over and he shone it under Bassman's van. Du Pré laid down and he reached under and picked something up. A black plastic canister, like a tiny fire extinguisher.

"Under there," said Booger Tom.

Du Pré handed it to him.

"She's good," said Booger Tom.

Du Pré nodded.

"She could be telling the truth maybe," said Du Pré.

"It don't make no sense," said Booger Tom.

Du Pré nodded. Truth don't make sense lots of times. Lots of times.

"God damn it," said Booger Tom. "It's that kid, I knows it."

Du Pré shrugged.

"The spray, it is tossed under the van," he said. "Maybe there was a person here, two maybe."

"But them tracks is all messed up," said Booger Tom.

Du Pré nodded.

"God damn it, Doo-Pray," said Booger Tom. "If you knows somethin' I don't, spit it out."

Du Pré shone the light on the ground again.

Booger Tom spat tobacco.

"I don't know," said Du Pré, "maybe could be a lot of things. So we have to wait."

Booger Tom snorted.

Du Pré stood up and he walked toward the open door in the side of the saloon.

CHAPTER

20

"I know what you think," said Julie. She mopped at her eyes with a sopping rag.

"Julie . . . ," said Bart, "we're trying to help."

"Your idea of fucking help, Uncle Bart, is paying some psychiatrist to tell you you were right and I need therapy."

Bart sighed.

"What should I do then?" he said.

Julie blinked at him, her eyeballs cherry red around the brown.

"I don't know," she said, "what you should do. I'm not old and wise enough. I get maced and Bassman gets clubbed and you think I *did* it. I *like* Bassman." Her eyes watered.

Du Pré rolled a smoke and lit it and he turned away.

Bart came to him, head down.

"Maybe Madelaine . . . ," he said.

"Uncle Bart," said Julie, "I'm not deaf. I just can't see well. I'll tell Madelaine the same thing. I didn't spray myself and I didn't club Bassman. Oh, what's the use?" She put the wet towel to her face and she got up and she groped for the door and she went outside.

Bart threw up his arms.

"I'm hopeless," he said. "I can't do anything right."

"Quit whining," said Madelaine, passing by. She went on out the door after Julie.

"Ah," said Du Pré, putting his hand on Bart's shoulder, "me . . . I got those two daughters . . . thing is . . . sometimes you can't do *anything* right. God would screw it up."

"Do you think she did it?" said Bart.

Du Pré shook his head.

"I thought you did," said Bart.

"I think maybe," said Du Pré, "but I don't now. Beck, he thinks, ver' straight line. Easy to walk, them."

Bart nodded.

"She's a good kid," said Bart, "and I can't for the life of me figure out what she needs."

Du Pré walked out the front door and he looked round. Allison Ames was sitting in her little white SUV, looking at Du Pré. She got out and she walked over slowly.

"Bassman's half killed," she said. "Kinda getting dirty. All over the lost journals. Julie gets maced. Maybe I'll do a book. Yeah, 'cause how long will it be, do you think, before somebody gets murdered. Lots of money there. People kill for lots of money."

Du Pré nodded.

He looked down at her feet. He reached for her right foot suddenly, and he lifted it and twisted it so he could see the sole of the light cloth-and-leather hiking boot.

Allison Ames struggled a little, her balance uncertain.

"Fucker," she hissed, "let go."

Du Pré pulled his hands away.

"I don't *do* it," said the reporter. "I *watch* it."

Du Pré looked at her for a long time.

"Your right leg, shorter than your left one," he said, "so you drag your left heel a little. Foot turns out some, too. So you been at Benetsee's. Been lots of places. Change your shoes. Get new ones. I still know it is you. Somebody hurt my friend. Somebody is playing games, wants the journals. Two people hurt, now. Watching, it is not good enough. Don't play fucking games with me. I go, say, Benny, that Ames woman her tracks are by Bassman's van, she is the one, you maybe sit in jail, Cooper, can't watch much."

Ames looked away.

"It wasn't me," she said. "I was inside, listening, and I had a soft drink after your set. I never went outside until the commotion started."

"Other reporters are there, yes?" said Du Pré.

"Three," said Ames. "Well, two for sure and another one maybe."

"Who?" said Du Pré.

"There was a big heavy guy who was acting drunk but wasn't. Had a brown leather coat on . . ."

Du Pré nodded.

"A woman in drugstore cowboy duds, had opals on her hatband . . ."

Du Pré nodded.

"Benson Drew," said Ames, "he writes for an online magazine. *Sheet.* I haven't met him. He just got here this afternoon."

Du Pré looked at her.

"Young kid, looks like a . . . yuppie mountain climber," said Ames.

"Bassman dies," said Du Pré, "him die, my good friend, I will be ver' angry. Ver' angry. So. Maybe you tell me what you see."

Ames spread her hands.

"I have tried to see the old medicine man," she said. "The journals are a big story. Very big. The bicentennial of the Lewis and Clark journey is soon upon us."

Du Pré waited.

"I get a old violin, worth a fortune," said Du Pré, "tells me I got to talk to them, but I don't. Who are they?"

Ames shrugged.

"Bullshit," said Du Pré, "maybe you tell them no but they find you, yes?"

Ames looked off. She nodded.

"Who is it?" said Du Pré.

"Some computer wizard," said Ames. "I got an offer, it just popped up on the screen. Hundred grand. Just for finding where the journals *are.*"

"Who?" said Du Pré.

"I gave what I had to a guy at the paper," said Ames, "I mean the *Wall Street Journal.*"

"What him do with it?"

"He tried to find out who sent it and just hit a wall. This guy is very, very good. I am not computer genius, but it seems he finds a new route each time he contacts anyone, and then he erases his tracks. Not all of them, sometimes three or four connections can be traced, but then there isn't anything."

Du Pré nodded. He rolled a cigarette.

"Don't play games, me," he said, "play like a goddamned lawyer. Who you *think* is doing this?"

Ames looked at her watch. It was a quick movement, and then she cleared her throat.

Du Pré grabbed her by the arm and he dragged her into the saloon and back to the kitchen. Bart was there, sitting on a stool, looking lost.

"Her," said Du Pré, "keep her here. She gives you shit, throw her in the freezer, goddamn bitch."

Bart looked puzzled.

"I don't got time, explain," said Du Pré.

Ames yelled a few things at Du Pré and Bart stood up, massive and red-faced.

"*Shut up!*" he roared.

Du Pré ran back outside and he got in Bassman's van and he started it and he backed and turned and he drove up to the far end of town and he turned on the road that led to his old place where Raymond and Jacqueline and their twelve kids lived now.

Du Pré went to a big shed and he slid the door open and then he drove Bassman's van in and he cut the engine and he began to root around in the van, tossing bags of marijuana into a paper sack. He pulled out the little drawers under the back seats and he rifled the glove box and he checked behind the sun visors.

"Du Pré," said Raymond, looking very sleepy, "you are doing what?"

"I got to get all Bassman's dope the fuck out of his van," said Du Pré. "Him, been set up I think."

"I help?" said Raymond.

"Yah," said Du Pré. "Crawl under maybe see there is something stuck the frame."

Du Pré started again at the back doors and he worked his way forward. He pulled at the carpets but they were tight and the steel floor solid under them. He checked every little place again.

"Yah," said Raymond. "Under here . . ."

Du Pré knelt down and Raymond handed him a plastic bag full of white powder, about a half cup.

"This is not Bassman," said Du Pré.

"What is that?" said Raymond.

"Speed maybe," said Du Pré, "don't matter what, there is a lot here."

"Why somebody do this, Bassman?" said Raymond.

Du Pré shrugged.

"OK," said Du Pré, giving Raymond the little bag. "You burn this bag, everything, all burnt, the grass you hide someplace. I got to take this damn van back now."

Raymond went off.

Du Pré backed out and he drove down the street to the Toussaint Saloon and he parked the van.

Madelaine and Julie were inside now, and Bart and Allison Ames were glaring at each other.

"Pret' shitty," said Du Pré.

"What?" said Allison Ames, looking innocent.

Cars pulled into the parking lot.

CHAPTER

21

"Damn it, Du Pré," said Harvey Wallace, Blackfeet and FBI, "I can't do anything. The fine folks at the Drug Enforcement Administration hate us FBI people, you know how it is, two dogs, one bone."

"Yah," said Du Pré, "three cars, twelve agents, they get this hot tip, dope in Bassman's van, drive three hundred miles, attack at dawn. Who calls them? Newspaper reporter. Bunch of speed, in this bag under Bassman's van, the frame."

"Shit happens all the time," said Harvey. "Lots of folks in the can got set up that way."

"Twelve agents?" said Du Pré.

"Does seem to be overkill," said Harvey.

"Bassman, him in the hospital, somebody crack his skull. He is in Billings. Why are there twelve agents, drive three hundred miles his van?"

"I dunno," said Harvey. "It's really out of my jurisdiction."

"Fine," said Du Pré. "You talk, Madelaine then . . ."

He handed the telephone to Madelaine.

"Blackfeet son of a bitch," said Madelaine, cooing, "you are giving Du Pré the me-I-don't-know, yes? We got our Bassman, you dance him plenty, in Billings they operate on his brain, somebody club him, and somebody stick some dope, his van frame, and call the drug cops and you tell me you don't know nothing?"

Madelaine smiled while Harvey talked at some length.

"Good," said Madelaine, "I call your wife then . . ."

Harvey began to talk louder.

"So fucking find out!" said Madelaine. "Shit, Du Pré him find out things for you, yes?"

Harvey said something really loud and he hung up.

"Him have to eat three jelly donuts," said Madelaine, "calm him down some there."

"You call his wife?" said Du Pré.

"Harvey don't call back two hours I call his wife," said Madelaine. "Fair is fair."

Madelaine yawned.

It was nine in the morning and neither she nor Du Pré had slept.

"So," said Madelaine.

The telephone rang and Madelaine picked up the old black receiver.

She listened.

"No shit," she said. "Him be all right then."

She listened some more.

"We come down," said Madelaine, "you call us first." She put the phone back in the cradle.

Du Pré sipped his ditch.

"They operate on Bassman," said Madelaine. "Not too bad Kim says. She is sitting by the bed, sees his eyes move a little. She leans over, so she can hear. Bassman, him say ver' loud, I AM NOT GET-TING NO FUCKING JOB."

Du Pré snorted.

"Bassman him look good," said Madelaine.

Du Pré shook his head.

"Why him?" said Du Pré.

"We go sleep and then we ask *why him?*" said Madelaine.

"Yah," said Du Pré.

They went out and got in Du Pré's old cruiser. Bassman's van sat

102

where it had been when the DEA agents came, and there were scraps of foam from the seat padding here and there. The agents had slit every seat cover and torn up all of the carpeting. They had ripped down the velour from the ceiling. They had gotten angrier and angrier when they found nothing at all.

"Poor Bassman," said Madelaine.

"Him do all right," said Du Pré. "Julie she is out there with her video filming the agents, pissing them off. Him get a new van, probably."

"Maybe they stick on a new head, the hospital," said Madelaine. "Him need that more."

Du Pré snorted.

"Kim, she is good for him," said Madelaine, "the poor son of a bitch."

"Damn Benetsee get rid of those journals," said Du Pré, "this maybe all get quiet."

He parked in front of her house and they went in and fell into bed and both were asleep like that.

Du Pré woke up suddenly, hearing a voice.

"No shit," said Madelaine. "Jesus. Government peckerheads."

Du Pré yawned and he sat on the bed and began to pull on his clothes.

She came into the bedroom.

"Some informant," said Madelaine, "said Bassman had his van mostly packed with methamphetamine. Harvey say 'reliable informant' then he laugh. And he say after they give him the bullshit, guy whispers that the tip came in on the computer, Billings, no telephone call."

"World," said Du Pré, "is so much better place since they got computers."

"Same people," said Madelaine, "trying to get those journals I bet."

Du Pré yawned. He got thick strong coffee.

"They don't club Bassman, though," he said.

Madelaine nodded.

"Me," she said, "I can't think that one out. Why hit Bassman? Him don't know nothing. Why take Julie?"

Du Pré sucked down a heavy load of the coffee.

"Maybe Beck got more now," he said.

Madelaine began to fry eggs and make toast.

They ate without talking.

They went back to bed and got up and Madelaine let Du Pré shower first because he was fast and she was very slow.

They drove back down to the saloon.

Susan Klein was there pulling beers for the old men who came in in the afternoon.

"Fun night," she said, looking at Du Pré and Madelaine.

Susan put an envelope down in front of Du Pré. Du Pré sighed and he opened it.

He read the odd print.

Madelaine looked at the paper.

"It was on the window ledge by the stage," said Susan, "under a drink. Behind the curtain. Left last night, I guess."

"Ten million dollars for the journals," said Madelaine, "and five million more if they are real."

"I've had it," said Susan. "Go get the fuckers and I will be rich if you don't like the idea. I'd sell those suckers like that."

Du Pré looked at Madelaine.

"Julie, she is taking movies last night?" he said.

"Uh-huh," said Madelaine.

"Oh," said Susan, "Bart called and said to come out when you could. I think something about those movies she took last night."

"You go," said Madelaine, "I got to work. Susan has the dentist."

"I could go another time," said Susan.

Madelaine shook her head.

Du Pré waited while Susan made him a ditchwater highball in a white plastic go-cup and he went out and he got in his old cruiser and he drove off toward Bart's place.

It was getting hot.

Big stoneflies thwapped into the grill and the windshield.

Du Pré turned into the long road that led to the house. He saw Beck's big Suburban and Bart's pair of big green SUVs and the dented old Chevy that Booger Tom drove when he couldn't ride a horse.

104

They were all in front of the big TV set, looking at dark film of Du Pré and Bassman playing and then at some of the crowd.

Julie's eyes were a little pink but not angry-looking.

"Du Pré," said Paul Beck, "I believe we have a little more to go on."

Julie backed the film up.

The song Du Pré played ended and the camera moved to a knot of people off to the left of the little stage, past the window.

Allison Ames stood there, in big dark glasses.

A young man, blond and compactly built, stood near her. They did not speak, but then the young man walked past Ames and she looked at something in her hand for a moment before putting her hand in her jacket pocket.

"Warm in there for a coat," said Beck.

Du Pré nodded.

"You ever seen him before?" said Beck.

Du Pré shook his head.

"I wish I had shot more of the crowd," said Julie.

"So do we," said Beck, "but you didn't."

"We need to find that guy," said Beck.

"Allison Ames knows him," said Du Pré. "They talked once, he came to her car. I saw them."

"I wish," said Beck, "I knew what this was about."

CHAPTER

22

"I don't know who the guy is," said Ames. "I thought he was hitting on me. He gave me a note and I put it in my pocket and I tossed it without looking at it. I don't know when he came in and I don't know when he left and I don't know where he came *from.* Jesus."

Du Pré looked at Beck, who looked at Ames.

"Du Pré," said Beck, "let me talk to her alone."

Du Pré shrugged. He walked away from the big Suburban where the three of them had been sitting. Beck had a VCR in it, with a tiny little screen with a very good picture.

He was still tired from the long night before.

Ames got out of the Suburban, slamming the door, and she stalked away toward her little white SUV.

Du Pré ambled back to the big Suburban. Beck rolled down the window.

"I made it clear to her how much trouble we can cause her," said Beck, "which is not near enough. I would dearly like to get one good hold on what this mess is."

Du Pré nodded.

"What if I play their game?" he said.

"Offer up the journals?" said Beck. "We've talked about it—Foote and I and a few others in on this. These people are clever. I don't think they'd fall for it, and I don't think they'd let down their guard long enough for us to get to them."

"I have the journals," said Du Pré, "I think they have to come for them."

"Nope," said Beck, "they'll have some sort of cutout."

Du Pré looked at him.

"Use the U.S. Mail," said Beck, "have it sent express to one of those private PO Box places, have it forwarded from there. We can't mess with the mail. No, they want to have the journals but they want something else, too. I don't know what."

Du Pré sighed.

"I see you," he said.

He drove out to Bart's, and a couple of miles from the ranch he could see Julie in the air. The day was bright and still and Du Pré watched her bank and turn and head for the Wolf Mountains blue to the north.

Du Pré parked by the house. Booger Tom and Bart were drinking coffee and sitting on the deck. Du Pré got some for himself and he joined them.

"Had them things I was young I'd not be here," said Booger Tom.

"Tom thinks Julie is trying to commit suicide," said Bart.

"Yah," said Du Pré, sitting on the top step. The little ultralight aircraft turned and began to come toward the three sitting on the deck.

The snarl of the tiny engine began to grow.

Julie dipped and turned and came on.

The airstrip in the pasture had recently been graded and the orange windsock hung down.

Wind start in about an hour, Du Pré thought. Down from the mountains in the morning, then it gets still, then up toward them in the afternoon.

The little aircraft got closer and Julie began to lose altitude. She came into the graded part of the runway and she set the little machine down very gently. The engine noise died and the ultralight soon stopped and Julie unstrapped herself and she got out and she took off her helmet and she shook out her long dark hair.

Bart walked out toward the strip. By the time he got there Julie had broken the wings down and they pulled the machine to a shed and put it in and then they began to walk back.

Booger Tom spat at a beetle walking across the dust.

"She'll be a good horsewoman," he said. "She is gettin' to think like a horse does."

Du Pré nodded.

How you think with a prune, he thought. Horse brain, just that big.

"She's mighty upset," said Booger Tom, "that we all thought she was the one clubbed Bassman."

"It wasn't her," said Du Pré.

"We know that now," said Booger Tom, "but has anyone ever thought of apologizin'?"

"OK," said Du Pré.

"She's goin' back to town teach some of them little monsters how to be monkeys," said Booger Tom. "Maybe she's plottin' to whittle yer tribe down there."

Du Pré nodded.

Julie and Bart got close and Julie nodded at Du Pré and she went on in the house.

"I'm going to take her to town," said Bart, "and we'll have dinner at the saloon. She's going to teach some kids some gymnastics."

Du Pré got up. He stretched and he yawned and he went to his old cruiser and he got in and he drove off toward Benetsee's, taking the bench road to the rutted track that went up to the old man's cabin.

Du Pré smelled wood smoke as soon as he got close, and he went to the spot he usually parked in and he got out and he walked round behind the cabin and down the hill to the little meadow where the sweat lodge stood.

The door was shut and Du Pré sat on a stump and he waited.

Benetsee was singing, his old voice powerful.

Steam curled out from the edges of the old sleeping bag that covered the door.

More singing. Du Pré didn't know the language.

The flap came up and the old man stepped out naked but for a ragged old pair of shorts and he scuffled to the edge of the pool in the creek and he jumped in. Du Pré waited. He rolled a smoke and he lit it and he took a deep drag.

The cigarette was plucked from his fingers. Benetsee was behind him, dressed now. Du Pré went back to his car and he got the wine from the trunk and he took a jar from the porch and he went back down to the stump he had been sitting on. Benetsee was there now. Du Pré poured him some wine.

"Old man," said Du Pré, "nothing is clear."

Benetsee drank. He nodded.

"You take the writings now, the other things," said Benetsee. "I got to go, Canada." He got up and he went up the hill to his cabin and he went in and he came back out with a cardboard box that once held bananas.

Du Pré took it.

Benetsee looked at him for a long time.

"One person is dead now," he said, "one more soon. Ver' bad this."

Du Pré looked at him.

"Who?" he said.

Benetsee shrugged.

He went into the cabin, leaving Du Pré with the box in his hands.

Du Pré went to his cruiser and he put the box in the trunk. He lifted the lid and saw the packages wrapped with plastic, clear sheets. Some journals, a little lead canister, an astrolabe, rusty tools.

He drove back to Toussaint and he went to the saloon. Madelaine was behind the bar, beading.

Du Pré went to the stool in front of her.

"Benetsee says one person is dead, there will be another," said Du Pré.

"Nobody dead I heard of," said Madelaine. "Old bastard come for dinner maybe?"

Du Pré shook his head.

"Him go to Canada," he said.

Madelaine nodded.

"He don't say who is dead?" she said.

Du Pré shook his head. He came round the bar and he made himself a ditchwater highball.

He went back to his stool. Madelaine held a bead up to the light, stuck on her needle. She made a quick stitch.

"What you think Du Pré?" said Madelaine.

Du Pré shook his head.

"Ames woman she is lying, what I think," he said.

Madelaine nodded.

"Enough money people lie pret' good," she said.

Du Pré nodded.

"Julie don't got nothing to do with this," said Madelaine. "I would know she did."

Du Pré had some of his drink.

The pay phone rang. Du Pré went to answer it.

"Gabriel," said the dispatcher, the woman who hated Du Pré, "Benny wants you to come out to the big gravel pit. The highway pit out west there."

Du Pré hung the telephone back up.

"One?" said Madelaine as he passed.

Du Pré nodded.

CHAPTER

23

Beck was already there when Du Pré turned off among the huge piles of fine gravel used to sand the roads in winter.

Benny was sitting in his cruiser, looking lost.

He rubbed his eyes when Du Pré walked up to the car. He got out and he led Du Pré and Beck behind the largest of the piles. There was a red Jeep Cherokee there. A man lay beside it, flies on his eyes and the little hole in his head.

Benny turned away.

Du Pré knelt and he looked at the body. There were some small marks where his feet had scuffed a little while he was dying, but he had died very fast.

The ground around was rough gravel, the same as the big pile.

A used condom lay under the man's right shoe.

Beck cleared his throat.

"Not much to hold tracks here," he said, "and a lot of cars turn in here, it seems."

Du Pré nodded. Kids come to fuck and drink beer.

"Benny," said Du Pré, "you call anybody?"

"Yah," said Benny, "I asked for the state police. This ain't some dead husband we know and the wife shot him, too."

Du Pré stood up.

"They get pissy we mess with it," he said. He went to the Cherokee and he looked in it. The windows were all down. There was a small flat bag on the passenger seat. Du Pré lifted it up and he looked at the luggage tag.

"Benson Drew," said Du Pré, "San Francisco."

"Let me see that," said Beck. Du Pré handed it to him. Beck undid the zipper and he slid out the laptop and he popped something and he pulled out a disc and he slid it in his pocket.

"They shit they find that out," said Du Pré.

"My job," said Beck, "is to protect Julie and Bart. Let 'em shit."

A siren sounded a long way off.

"That'll be McPhie," said Benny, "securin' the crime scene. He can have it."

"Benny don't like murders," said Du Pré.

Beck shrugged.

He opened the passenger door and he looked in the glove box and in an attaché case he picked up from the floor. He took some more discs out and then he went to his Suburban.

Beck drove off.

Du Pré and Benny waited.

The Highway Patrol cruiser topped a hill, light bar flashing. In a few moments McPhie was turning into the gravel dump. He drove up to Benny's car and he stopped and got out.

"What we got?" he said. McPhie was huge, and he walked like a bear.

Benny pointed.

McPhie looked down at the body.

"Neat," he said. "I am sure you haven't touched anything?"

"No," said Du Pré.

"No," said Benny.

"They get awful hinky you touch somethin'," said McPhie. "They got all that fancy shit, electronic tape measures and such. Lookin' at the deceased here, it seems that who done it knew what they were doing."

Du Pré nodded.

"Who found him?" said McPhie.

"Carl was flyin' over checkin' his cows," said Benny. "Said he didn't notice the body goin' out cause it was in a shadow but he seen it comin' back. Radioed it in."

McPhie nodded.

"Dispatcher'll have the time," said Benny.

"Well," said McPhie, "he ain't from around here for sure."

Du Pré nodded.

"I will be home," he said. He walked to his old cruiser and he got in and he drove back to Toussaint. The saloon was busy now and Madelaine was rushing back and forth setting people up. Du Pré made himself a ditch and he sat at the end of the bar.

Madelaine finished for a moment and she came, one eyebrow raised.

"Journalist," said Du Pré. "Allison Ames said his name."

Madelaine nodded.

"One shot the head," said Du Pré.

Madelaine looked at him.

Someone down the bar called out her name and she went to get them what they wanted.

Du Pré saw Beck at the kitchen port. He must have come in through the back. He motioned, and Du Pré picked up his drink and he went on back. Beck waited past the prep counter in the center of the room.

"Drew wrote for a computer magazine, one that is actually on the computer," said Beck. "And I haven't got all the way through those discs—but his office says he called in early this morning saying he had to see a source and he would have the story."

Du Pré nodded.

"What story?" he said.

"The LESA Corporation," said Beck. "It's a specialized software company, started by some genius named Markham Milbank. Milbank is quite eccentric, and he loves to play games."

Du Pré looked at Beck.

"He likes to buy expensive things and donate them to museums and take the tax breaks," said Beck.

Du Pré nodded.

"That's what I recall," said Beck. "The discs are all transferred to Chicago where they will sort them out."

"Why him kill this guy?" said Du Pré.

Beck shook his head.

"Not his style. He's not a crook and never has been. He has a whole lot of money and enough so he needs his own security people. Apparently Drew got wind of the fun Markham was having up here and he came so he would be next to the journals when they surfaced."

Du Pré nodded.

In the banana box, the trunk of my cruiser.

"I'll know more in a while," said Beck, "about that. You got any ideas?"

Du Pré shook his head.

"I don't know," he said. "Bassman gets clubbed, Julie gets sprayed with that shit, Drew ends up dead, why? None of them got the journals. None of them have anything to do with them. Bart doesn't have them."

"Who does?" said Beck.

"Benetsee," said Du Pré, "him got them hid someplace."

"The medicine man," said Beck.

Du Pré nodded.

"Will he ever be back?" said Beck.

Du Pré nodded.

"Day after tomorrow," he said.

Some small electronic beeper began to sound. Beck went out the back door to his Suburban. He got in and picked up the telephone. He bent over, listening.

Du Pré rolled a smoke and he waited.

Beck put the telephone down and he leaned over the passenger seat for a moment and then he got out. He was shaking his head.

"Nothing," he said. "Old stories. Couple blanks. Nothing at all about this." Beck waved at the country.

Du Pré sipped his drink.

"So what we do?" he said.

"Keep an eye on Julie and Bart," said Beck. "Damned Bart, I could sure use some more people. He hates having us underfoot."

Du Pré nodded.

He went back into the saloon. He went out and he got in his cruiser and he drove to his old place. Kids shrieked happily behind the house, where the huge jungle gym was. Du Pré walked back and he looked at Julie, her hands on Pallas's waist, explaining something to her.

Bart looked over.

"She's a good teacher," he said.

"Beck wants more people," said Du Pré. "Maybe you better do that."

Bart flushed.

"This is not something I know," said Du Pré. "Makes no sense."

Bart threw up his hands and he went off toward his big SUV.

Pallas was on top of the jungle gym. She dropped down and she grabbed a crossbar and she flexed her body and pulled her legs up and she pivoted around the bar.

"That's right!" said Julie, "way to go!"

Pallas grinned widely. Her eyeteeth were missing.

She clambered back up the bars and she stood upright on top.

"Don't get cocky!" said Julie. "Pay attention!"

CHAPTER
24

"Benson is dead?" said Allison Ames. "As in, someone *killed* him?"

"That's right," said Benny Klein, "and I have to ask you where you were yesterday."

"I was in Cooper for a while," said Ames, "and I drove around up toward the Wolf Mountains."

Benny nodded.

"If you leave," he said, "I will wonder. Lots of folks will wonder. You newspeople don't exactly stick together."

"We're in competition," said Ames. "We don't kill each other."

"Now this Drew feller wrote for some . . . thang on the computer," said Benny, "a whatchacallit."

"Magazine," said Ames.

"Magazine is a paper usually got pictures in it," said Benny, "but never mind. So he was here doin' what?"

"A story on Markham Milbank," said Ames. "He owns the LESA corporation. They do software."

"Where is that Milbank feller?" said Benny.

"Austin, Texas," said Ames.

"So why wasn't this Drew feller in Austin, Texas?" said Benny.

Ames shook her head.

"He the feller keeps leaving money around, lots of money, and wants them journals ol' Du Pré found?" said Benny.

"Drew thought so," said Ames.

"So him and you did talk a bit," said Benny.

Ames nodded.

"This Milbank feller have him killed?" said Benny.

"Look," said Ames, "this is all speculation. I have no idea who would want to kill Drew. No idea. Milbank would hardly kill Drew. How would that help him get the journals?"

"What's he want 'em for?" said Benny.

"He buys rare things and gives them to museums," said Ames.

"A rich wing nut," said Benny.

"Yeah," said Ames.

"What you think?" said Benny, looking at Du Pré.

Du Pré shrugged.

"She don't kill Drew," said Du Pré. "She is left-hand."

"Oh," said Benny.

"Person kill Drew is right-hand," said Du Pré. "Also very good. They shoot Drew once in the head with a twenty-two. Probably they have done that before."

"God," said Ames, "who would kill a writer over a story?"

"Writer found out something killer'd rather keep quiet, I expect," said Benny. "Look, we have to ask these questions, you see, and I am sorry fer upsettin' you. Have to find out what ol' Drew was up to the last few days of his life. Didn't look so old to me. Twenty-eight, his driver's license says."

Ames nodded.

Madelaine came round the bar and she gave a small snifter of brandy to Ames, who held it, looking like she didn't know what it was.

Benny stood up. He leaned over the table, his knuckles flat on the scarred wooden top.

"I don't like murderin' goin' on in my county," he said. "If you know anything or hear anything, you'd best speak up." He put his hat on and he went out the front door.

117

Allison Ames sipped her brandy. She shook her head once and she closed her eyes and put her right hand to them.

Ames looked up at Du Pré and she took her hand away from her face.

"Interrogations here are unusual," she said, trying to smile.

"He got the rubber hoses, back, there," said Madelaine. "What Benny said we all mean. Somebody is playin' dumb games, that Mildick or whatever his name is. You know how, get hold of Mildick?"

"He's a recluse," said Ames, "very eccentric."

"Eccentric," said Madelaine. "Asshole what he is. These dumb rich people got tons of money, they say, here is a million, get me this thing, and people get killed. It is Mildick's fault, this."

"Not legally," said Ames.

"Rich people write laws," said Madelaine. "Do that about as well as they do anything else."

"I don't know," said Ames. "I would think Mr. Fascelli's people would be able to reach Milbank."

Du Pré went out the front door and to his old cruiser and he took out the odd little telephone he hated and he punched some numbers in and he waited.

"Foote, please," said Du Pré when the woman answered.

"He is out at the moment," she said. "He will be back in ten minutes."

"It is Du Pré," said Du Pré. "I am at the saloon, Toussaint." He gave her the numbers.

Allison Ames was sitting at the bar having a second brandy when Du Pré came back in. She had some color in her cheeks now.

Madelaine stuck a platter with a cheeseburger and fries and coleslaw on it in front of Du Pré. He ate like a starving wolf. The platter was clean in three minutes.

"Glad I don't stick my hand in there," said Madelaine.

"I miss it," said Du Pré, "I aim my teeth good."

"I just want to write a story about the journals," said Allison Ames. "That's all."

"It is not the story you wanted?" said Madelaine. "So write about the one that is there, eh? Whining, don't help."

"No," said Ames, "it doesn't. I'm tired. I am going to my room over in Cooper and rest."

She went out.

The telephone rang and Du Pré answered it.

"Gabriel," said Charles Foote, who ran Bart's life better than he could.

"Yah," said Du Pré, "there is this Milbank man, LESA company, him around this bad stuff here."

"Markham Milbank," said Foote. "We are trying to reach him. It is not easy. We keep notching up the threats."

"OK," said Du Pré.

"He doesn't like to talk to anyone," said Foote. "We get a mouthpiece and in time another. Events around there do trace back to Milbank's unwise little games. He has, heretofore, not caused much trouble with them, so he assumed like we all do that life would go on as it had."

"I have the journals," said Du Pré.

"Tell me you're lying," said Foote, quickly.

"April fool," said Du Pré. "I don't got them."

"So," said Foote, "when we finally do get through to Milbank do you have any messages for him?"

"Yah," said Du Pré. "Quit fucking around, maybe, uh?"

"I will see that he gets it," said Foote.

"Beck, him say he needs more people," said Du Pré.

"Bart said no," said Foote. "He said that most forcefully."

Du Pré thought a moment.

"OK," he said. "I need something I call you."

"Gabriel," said Foote, "thanks. Bart has a point. Julie is not at all involved in this, and he really doesn't want to be stumbling over operatives all the time. Beck's damned good, and if he needs help he can get it in a hurry."

"OK," said Du Pré.

"Bassman is doing very well," said Foote. "I think he'll be coming back in a few days."

Du Pré and Foote said goodbye and hung up.

Du Pré sat across the bar from Madelaine and her beadwork.

"Bassman is better, come back in a couple days," said Du Pré.

Madelaine put her tongue in the corner of her mouth and she squinted at the bead on the needle.

"Old-age shit," she said. She put the needle through the soft leather.

"Bassman, him need a place to rest," said Madelaine, "so the Kleins' back trailer there we will have ready for him, Kim."

"Never hurt him hitting the head," said Du Pré.

"You got ideas, Du Pré, what this is about?" said Madelaine.

Du Pré shook his head.

"Not much," he said.

"What you going to do? Benetsee is gone, yes?" said Madelaine.

Du Pré looked at the ceiling.

"Hunt a coyote," he said.

Madelaine nodded.

"Smart coyote," said Madelaine.

"Smart coyote got to eat sometime," said Du Pré.

"Drink, too," said Madelaine.

Du Pré rolled a smoke and he lit it and he passed it to Madelaine, who took a long, deep drag.

Madelaine blew out a long blue stream of tobacco.

"Hunt him, Du Pré," she said.

CHAPTER

25

Du Pré put the green bananas on top of the journals and the old tools and the lead canister and he put the lid back on and he put the box in the cooler under two crates of lettuce.

"Don't mess my bananas," he said to Madelaine when he came out.

"I mess your banana any damn time I want," said Madelaine, "but I tell Susan forget they are in there."

"OK," said Du Pré.

"So," said Madelaine, "what you do now?"

Du Pré yawned.

"Me," he said, "I think I go a bunch of places, look around. I got a couple questions, got to check Benetsee's place, he is gone, you know."

He went out and got in his old cruiser and he drove off toward the old man's cabin. He stopped at the turn onto the rutted track from the county road and he looked for a long time at the ground before he drove up to the cabin. He parked in the tall weeds and he sauntered around the empty cabin. The sweat lodge was open and the firepit cold a long time.

A kingfisher flew down the creek, a little silver trout in its bill.

Du Pré looked the ground over carefully. He went to the cabin and he stuck hairs on the door, one high and one low, with spit. He got down on his knees and looked along the sagging porch and then he went back to his car and he got in and he drove down to the country road and then west toward the north-south highway.

The day was beautiful, sunny and bright with high white cottony clouds cast across the blue. A light plane flew over, and began to lose altitude, heading for the grassy strip at Cooper.

Du Pré turned around at the crossroads and he got up to one-ten quickly and he turned off on a side road and he headed up to Bart's place, on the benchland that reached out six miles or so from the Wolf Mountains.

Julie was in the air when Du Pré got there, the tiny little aircraft, maroon and blue and yellow, moving slowly a couple of hundred feet above the ground.

Du Pré got out and he walked round back of the house and he squinted up at Julie.

"Durn girl tried to get me to fly that danged thing," said Booger Tom. He went back to thinking about maybe doing that.

"I blow you out of the sky, a shotgun," said Du Pré. "What an old fart like you want to do that for?"

"I knowe'd you'd understand," said Booger Tom. "Bart's round puttin' a hose on the backhoe. I tol' him twenty times he can't reach that far with the bucket, but he don't listen."

"Bart," said Du Pré, "him like putting hoses on maybe."

Booger Tom snorted.

Du Pré found Bart happily inserted in the innards of the big backhoe.

"What you find there, Bart?" said Du Pré.

"Meaning . . . of . . . life," said Bart. He twisted something and he put his hand out and Du Pré gave him the socket wrench.

"Julie is pret' good that thing," said Du Pré.

"Sure is," said Bart. "She has such incredible balance. She's a good, cautious kid, too, you know, thinks about everything. Pilots who don't are in the ground."

"How come you won't get people here, help Beck?" said Du Pré.

"We talked about it," said Bart. "He couldn't really convince me that we needed more. He said this Markham Milbank clown was the culprit and they'd take care of it."

"Him know that?" said Du Pré.

"Foote did," said Bart. "Look, if I knew there was a danger I would of course take steps. But Julie is fine and has no part in this, and so am I, and I have no part in this, nor do any of my friends and my neighbors. That reporter, Drew, I gather, had a genius for enraging people."

"OK," said Du Pré.

"I can't live my life surrounded by armed guards," said Bart. He twisted something and yelped.

He backed out of the mess of black hoses and yellow metal and he looked at the blood welling from his left forefinger.

Du Pré went to get the first aid kit. He bandaged the wound, tight.

Booger Tom came in to the machine shed.

"Benny Klein just called," said Booger Tom, "an' some character name of Milbank landed in Cooper half hour ago or so and is raising hell to see Du Pré and Bart. I was you, I'd go to Vegas for the weekend."

Du Pré and Bart looked at each other.

"Son of a bitch," said Bart. "The little turd is here."

Du Pré went out the sliding door. Bart followed.

"So," said Bart, "what do we do?"

"I drive you that thing," said Du Pré, nodding at the dark-green SUV. "You act like I am your hired driver."

Bart nodded. He looked at Julie, a bright speck in the air up toward the mountains.

They got in Bart's Lincoln and Du Pré took the drop road down and he turned and headed for Cooper. The highway was clear and the big SUV nearly left the road past eighty, so it took them longer than it would have in Du Pré's old cruiser to get there.

There was a huge motor home parked in front of the little grocery store, blocking the entire length of the building, and on the wrong side of the street.

"That'll be him," said Bart. "It's the grace of new money."

Du Pré snorted. He parked well away from the wheeled condo.

Bart wandered up the street in his oily coveralls, Du Pré a few paces behind.

There was a wispy young man in thick horn-rimmed glasses standing by the door in the side of the motor home. He was drinking Poland Spring mineral water.

"Markham Milbank about?" said Bart, amiably.

The young man regarded Bart's greasy, stained, worn appearance. "And you are?" he said.

"Bart Fascelli," said Bart, "and I could write a check for his entire chickenshit operation and I may if he don't get his ass out here."

"Good God," said the youngster, backing away. He went into the motor home. He was soon back.

"Milbank would like to know what you want," he said.

"I want to talk to him," said Bart. "I'm psychotic, you see, and if I am thwarted, I tend to spray the entire area with bullets and get off on technicalities."

"OK," said the young man, going back into the motor home. He came back quickly. Du Pré was standing by Bart.

"He'll see you," said the young man, opening the door.

Bart and Du Pré went on up the steps and into the main room, which was spare and bleak and had a few computer consoles on stands here and there. There were several posters for rock band concerts on the walls and a paper mobile in the center of the room.

The young man went round behind a small black desk and he pointed to some weird-looking chairs. Bart and Du Pré stood.

"I'm Markham Milbank," said the young man.

Bart nodded.

The door opened and two other young men came in.

"Jerry!" barked Milbank. "God damn it. We aren't fucking royalty and if we were it is no excuse to act like this. Get the damn thing on the right side of the street and out of other people's way. Jesus! Christ!"

The two young men went swiftly toward the front of the motor home and the engine came to life and it lumbered slowly off.

"What the fuck," said Bart.

Milbank held up a hand.

"It is my responsibility," he said. "I stupidly indulged myself in playing games with people and now someone is dead, I suspect because of the very large offer I made for the journals and artifacts. I had no idea anyone would . . . kill for things of interest only to scholars."

"I think," said Bart, "the interest is in the money."

"Isn't it always," said Milbank. "I have so much I don't even know how much I have. I have given away four hundred million dollars and hardly made a dent."

"So," said Bart, "why are you here?"

"I seem to have erred," said Milbank. "I'd like to make it as right as I can."

The motor home had stopped.

The two young men came back, and then a man in his fifties came from a room at the back.

"My vice-presidents," said Milbank, "Jerry Soldner and Pat Henkel, and the gentleman behind you is Torbert Thommassen, who is my chief of security."

Bart shook hands with them all.

Markham Milbank turned.

"And," he said, "you must be Gabriel Du Pré."

CHAPTER

26

"Tor and I worked out of the San Diego office," said Beck. He raised his glass to his friend.

"Did some work together," said Torbert Thommassen.

They were at the bar of the saloon, each with a large martini.

"War stories," said Markham Milbank. "Excuse me, I got to go and oil my duck."

Thommassen and Beck laughed and put their heads together again.

Julie kept looking at the front door of the saloon. Conor and his father were due in any time.

Du Pré looked down the bar and he sat back. He was tending the customers while Madelaine and Susan gave the trailer out back a last going over.

Bassman was coming, too. And Kim, the faithful burlap blonde.

Milbank went to a table and he sat alone, looking at the pages of an actual book.

The door opened again and Conor Burrows rushed in and Julie rose up from her chair and they each took three long steps and hugged, Julie pulling up her feet and Conor whirling her around.

Some other people came in behind them and they looked and grinned and found tables and the men came to the bar and ordered the drinks.

Du Pré pulled beers and he made whiskey ditches, good strong ones.

Friday night.

"Music tonight," said a rancher, "any chance?"

Du Pré shrugged.

"Maybe," he said. "Bassman, depend on how he feel, he get here." The rancher nodded and went off.

Du Pré looked up to see Eamon Burrows standing there.

"A small whiskey," said Burrows, "and a water back."

Du Pré poured and he put the shot in front of Burrows and he got a small glass and filled it with cold water. Burrows tossed the shot and he took the water and drank half of it.

Du Pré looked at Conor and Julie. Beautiful, young, healthy, and utterly lost in each other.

Du Pré heard the back door open and he turned and in a moment Susan Klein came in and then Madelaine. They put some cleaning rags away and Du Pré moved out from the bar and he left it to the experts.

Conor and Julie went out the front door.

"Off to get ruptures together," said Eamon Burrows, "and ain't love grand? Silly little bastards. I oughta be grateful they don't run off to join the circus."

Eamon pointed to the stool next to Du Pré and Du Pré nodded. Eamon looked off, lost in thought for a moment.

"Double bourbon on the rocks," he said to Madelaine.

"We got scotch," said Madelaine.

"How did you know?" said Eamon Burrows.

Madelaine laughed and she made his drink and got the money. She put it in the till.

"I was young once," said Burrows, "I think. So were you."

"Long time gone," said Du Pré.

"So what do you think of all this?" he said. "I worry about Julie.

127

That was a very bad business, when she got maced and that other fellow was clubbed."

Du Pré nodded.

"And no one knows who did it?" said Burrows.

Du Pré shook his head.

The door opened and Bassman came in, walking a bit slowly. His head was shaved and he had a bandage on the back of it. Kim followed, carrying his bass case.

"I help them," said Du Pré.

"Me, too," said Burrows. They went out to the van and got the amplifier and speakers and suitcase of odds and ends. The stench of marijuana was thick.

"Jesus," said Burrows, "I may fall over."

They pushed the stuff through the doors and over to the stage. Bassman and Kim were waiting.

"Give you new brain?" said Du Pré.

"*Non,*" said Bassman, "put new plugs and points, the old one. Man, I had some fuckin' headache."

Kim looked away.

"You hit him?" said Du Pré.

"I am beginning to wish I had," said Kim. "He seems to think I want him to get a job. He has a job. Making music."

"She don't mean it," said Bassman. "She is just waiting, say, Bassman, you go now get a nice job."

Du Pré set up Bassman's equipment. He got a chair and he put it where Bassman usually stood.

"I am sorry," said Bassman. "I stand too long I get dizzy."

"You play that good bass," said Du Pré. "Don't care you lie down. You lie down some anyway."

"Not beginning the evening," said Bassman.

Kim threw up her hands and she went to the bar and began to talk to Madelaine.

"One thing," said Bassman, "my strap, it is on the dingus next, the steering wheel."

Du Pré nodded and he went out to the van and he reached in and grabbed the strap. When he got back out Markham Milbank was standing there.

Milbank looked around and he nodded to a shadow by the out-buildings. He walked there swiftly, Du Pré after him.

"There's something about this that doesn't make sense," said Milbank. "I can't see it. Tor and that other guy are in there telling war stories. There is someone playing a double game and I can't figure out who. It isn't me. I am appalled that your friend got hurt."

Du Pré looked at him.

"Games," he said. "There is a lot of money, people start playing for blood."

"God," said Milbank, "what can I do? I don't even know who to trust. Could it be our own security people, for God's sake? I pay mine well. I can't find a crack. I can't see anything and I'm good at seeing things . . ."

"You want them journals," said Du Pré. "You are leaving money. Lots of money. You send me that violin. Books. Leave big cash. Some people, they maybe want that money."

"Tor hasn't got a goddamned reason to steal ten grand," said Milbank, "or fifty. It wouldn't be worth it, for God's sake."

Du Pré shrugged.

"I screwed up," said Milbank. "I want to make it right. What do I do?"

Du Pré didn't say anything.

"Something," said Milbank.

Du Pré rolled a smoke.

"Those guys with you," he said, "who are they?"

"Pat and Jerry?" said Milbank. "They have millions. They have stock."

Du Pré nodded.

"Somebody," said Du Pré, "is very dangerous. They kill this reporter. That is not a game. He is dead. Twenty-two in the head."

"God," said Milbank.

"Them journals," said Du Pré. "Ten million dollars. Lot of money, ten million dollars."

"I'd pay more," said Milbank, "they are priceless. I wanted to donate them to the National Archives. That is our epic. That journey."

"How much you pay?" said Du Pré.

"What do you mean?" said Milbank.

"You are asked for fifty million," said Du Pré, "you pay that?"

Milbank nodded.

"They are priceless," he said.

"So," said Du Pré, "you pay anything asked."

Milbank shrugged.

"Go home," said Du Pré. "Get these people of yours out of here and go home. You are not helping."

Milbank looked at Du Pré.

"All right," he said.

"Go now," said Du Pré.

Milbank shook his head.

"I want to hear you play," he said. "I have a couple of your tapes."

Du Pré nodded.

"Then you go," he said.

"Tor could stay," said Milbank. "He's damned good."

Du Pré shook his head.

"All right," said Milbank, "we'll leave right after you're done."

Du Pré finished his cigarette and he dropped it on the ground and he stepped on it.

They went back inside.

Thommassen and Beck were still talking and laughing. Pat and Jerry, the vice presidents, were drinking colas.

Du Pré went back to his stool.

He sipped on his ditch, and then he took it to the stage and he got on and Père Godin came in, carrying his accordion case.

They turned up and began to play. Bassman was just a little slower but not enough to matter.

Du Pré fiddled and sang, and the crowd finally got up and began to dance on the tiny floor. Julie and Conor held each other close, barely moving.

> . . . *black forest, black water, long time gone* . . .
> . . . *long time gone* . . .

Du Pré kept the tunes and tempos a little slower than usual. Bassman seemed fine but he was probably tired.

They finished and the lights in the saloon were turned up. It was a few minutes past closing time.

Du Pré helped Bassman pack his stuff in his van.

The huge motor home owned by Milbank pulled away, and Thommassen's SUV after it.

"He might have helped," said Beck, watching.

"*Non,*" said Du Pré.

CHAPTER

27

Madelaine put Kim and Bassman in the spare room for the night and she went to the kitchen to make something to eat. Soon there was a baking smell.

Du Pré came in and he looked at the sheet of cookies. Madelaine took a spatula and she picked them up and set them on waxed paper to cool.

Kim came in.

"He's asleep," she said. "He gets tired easily. They said it might be like that for months."

Du Pré made himself a cup of coffee. He drank it down quickly and he got his jacket and hat.

"It is three o'clock in the morning," said Madelaine.

"I got something to look at," said Du Pré.

He went out and got in his cruiser and he drove off toward the bench road and Benetsee's. He turned in the rutted drive and he bounced up to the old cabin.

Allison Ames's little white SUV was there. Du Pré could see a flashlight inside. He got out and he shut the door carefully and he went to the porch and he sat and waited.

She opened the door and came out. Her light beam fell on Du Pré and she screamed.

Du Pré just sat.

"Jesus!" said Ames. "God. Look, I know I'm not supposed to be here."

"I arrest you," said Du Pré, standing up. "That breaking and entering."

"It was unlocked," said Ames. She eyed the distance to her SUV.

Du Pré pulled handcuffs from his pocket.

"Jesus," said Ames, "Benson was a friend of mine. He was a good guy and now he's dead."

"You do this much," said Du Pré, nodding at Benetsee's cabin, "you will be dead, too. You think they won't kill you?"

"Why?" said Ames. She sat down on the porch steps.

Du Pré rolled a smoke.

"Money," he said.

"I want those journals," said Ames. "I want that story."

"You are pret' stupid," said Du Pré. "Come out here, poke around, you are alone. That Benson guy, he does that, too, he gets shot, one shot, twenty-two."

Allison Ames put her hands to her face.

Du Pré snapped one handcuff on her left wrist and he pulled her up and spun her round and grabbed her right wrist and pulled it back and snapped the other handcuff on her right wrist.

"You son of a bitch!" Ames screamed. "God damn you!" Then she began to cry.

Du Pré put her in the back of his old cruiser and he drove to Cooper and he went to the jail. He put Ames in a cell and she yelled and Du Pré shrugged and he walked out and left a note on the desk. There was no one there and there wouldn't be for several hours.

He drove back to Toussaint and then out to Bart's. There was a light on in the house.

Bart was sitting up, with Booger Tom. They were playing cards.

Cribbage. Du Pré looked at the clock on the wall. Five-thirty. It was getting light out.

"Julie was supposed to be back in an hour," said Bart. He looked mournfully at the clock.

Du Pré laughed.

"I lent them my rig," said Bart.

Du Pré yawned. He went to the room that he rented from Bart and he sat on the bed and he began to pull off his boot.

Bart appeared in the doorway.

"You think they ran off again?" he said.

Du Pré put his foot on the floor.

He shrugged.

"For God's sake," said Bart, "some bad things have happened here. I can worry, can't I?"

Du Pré sighed.

"Come on," he said. They went out and got in Du Pré's cruiser and they drove off toward Toussaint.

Bart's big dark-green Lincoln SUV was parked behind one of the trailers Susan Klein used for motel rooms.

"They aren't old enough to—" said Bart.

"Go ahead," said Du Pré, "be an uncle. Go pound, the door."

Bart sat there.

The door opened and Julie and Conor came out, disheveled, and they looked at Bart and Du Pré sitting in the cruiser.

Julie put her hands to the heavens. She walked over, and Bart rolled down the window.

"I'm sorry, Uncle Bart," she said. "I would have called, but there aren't any telephones in the rooms."

"I'm going to send you home," said Bart.

"Uncle Bart . . . ," said Julie.

Bart got out and he stalked over to his SUV and he threw open the door and he got in.

Julie ran after him. She spoke to him through the open door and then she got in. They sat, talking.

Conor stood with his hands in his pockets, looking at the ground.

Du Pré looked at Eamon Burrows's Volvo parked down the way in front of another trailer.

Julie got back out of Bart's car, and she slammed the door. Julie and Conor talked for a few minutes and Conor shook his head, still looking at the ground. He went to his father's room and he tapped on the door and Eamon Burrows opened it, wearing just his pants.

"Christ," said Du Pré.

He got out and he went to Bart's SUV and he got in and Bart looked at him, his face red.

"Quit," said Du Pré. "They are good kids you quit now."

"Christ," said Bart, "I had Beck watching them and I know that he is. I just worry, for God's sakes. That Drew character ended up dead, and Markham Milbank isn't anyone I'd trust. Those goddamned journals. I wish to Christ you'd never found the fucking things."

"Beck?" said Du Pré.

"Yeah," said Bart, "he was supposed to take care of this, and then I couldn't reach him. I thought maybe he was away from his car or something, but he didn't answer at all."

"Christ," said Du Pré, "why you don't tell me this?"

"I . . . ," said Bart.

Du Pré jumped out of the SUV. He went to his cruiser and he picked up the radio microphone.

He jumped back out.

"What?" said Bart.

"Get somebody up there," said Du Pré, "find Beck's car."

"He's around here someplace," said Bart.

Du Pré looked at him.

Bart walked off and he picked up his telephone and he made a call.

"Carl will be here in a little bit," said Bart. "Beck isn't here?"

Du Pré walked round the Toussaint Saloon and he went across the road to the little airfield and he waited. A small silver plane appeared on the western horizon and it soon began to descend and it landed and taxied up to the limp windsock.

Du Pré climbed in and Carl looked at him.

"The roads the front range," said Du Pré.

Carl pulled around and he got up speed and the little plane lifted off. He flew toward the Wolf mountains.

"What color is it?" said Carl.

"Red," said Du Pré. "Big damn Suburban."

They flew one leg and Carl came back a half mile north of the first.

They went across the whole front of the Wolf Mountains.

Du Pré saw a flash of red on a logging road.

"There," he yelled.

Carl followed Du Pré's finger.

The big Suburban was parked back in the trees, and hard to see from any direction. There was enough light now.

Carl flew back to the little Toussaint field and he landed and Du Pré jumped out and he ran to his cruiser and he got in and he drove with Bart behind him and Benny far back, light bar flashing.

Du Pré came to the road that led up to the Wolfs through the forest. There was a gate. He opened it and went on through.

The Suburban was set against the trees.

Du Pré felt the hood.

Cold.

He looked at the ground.

Bart drove up and Benny came wallowing along behind him, in the police cruiser, with the siren blowing.

Du Pré circled the Suburban.

"Jesus," said Bart.

Du Pré nodded.

Benny came running up.

He looked in the big truck.

"He's just gone?" said Benny.

Du Pré nodded.

He bent down and picked up a little brass shell. He tossed it away.

"What was that?" said Benny.

"Too old," said Du Pré.

"What the hell is going on?" said Benny.

"I'll call Foote," said Bart.

CHAPTER

28

Du Pré put the telephone back on its cradle and he sighed.

He went to the bar and he sat.

"Somebody tell me what is goin' on?" said Benny Klein. He looked rumpled and sleepy. "If there's been another killin' or a kidnappin' as sheriff I think maybe I oughta know."

"What is going on, Uncle Bart?" said Julie.

"Look," said Eamon Burrows, "let me take Julie. She will be safe in Portland."

"I am not," said Julie, "going to Portland. No way. Forget it."

Du Pré sighed and he drank his coffee. It had brandy in it.

"We don't know," said Du Pré. "Beck is gone. It maybe means something and maybe it does not."

"What do you *think* it means?" said Bart.

"You want that," said Du Pré, "you call some pyschic. They got 900 numbers, the telephone, I don't know."

"Foote is sending more people," said Bart. "This is my fault. I should have let him do that sooner."

Julie went to Bart and she put her arms around him.

"Not everything," she said, "is your fault."

Bart nodded but he didn't look like he believed her. He looked at Du Pré.

"That little prick," said Bart, "went only as far as *Billings*?"

"Yah," said Du Pré. "Foote said he was there, rented some offices, he is messing away, maybe sending hired people."

"Who?" said Julie.

"Markham Milbank," said Bart. "And Beck is gone. That little shit, I'll—"

"Why he take Beck?" said Du Pré.

Bart shrugged.

"He's a very wealthy man," said Bart. "He made millions by his middle twenties, more millions after that. I doubt that much he has wanted in his life escaped him."

"Them journals," said Du Pré.

Bart nodded.

"No end of trouble," he said. "I wish...." But he didn't say it again.

Conor Burrows nodded toward the corner and he and his father went there and they talked with their heads very close together and finally Eamon threw up his hands and nodded.

They came back.

"Conor is staying," said Eamon. "He won't go to Portland if Julie won't and—"

"Who can blame him?" said Bart.

"Jesus," said Madelaine. "Some good sense finally. Maybe you all live to get false teeth after all."

They all laughed.

"You may have the guesthouse," said Bart, "if you keep up the schoolwork."

He looked at Du Pré.

"Foote's sending several men from the security agency," he said. "They'll be in this evening, the first ones anyway. Beck is one of their own and they mean to get him back."

Du Pré nodded.

Bart looked at Conor and Julie.

"You'll have to bear being guarded," he said. "There is something very dangerous here."

The youngsters nodded.

Du Pré finished his drink and he put his hat on and he went out to his old cruiser and he got in and he drove to the red SUV that Beck had last been seen in. He opened all of the doors and he looked carefully under the seats and through the few papers in the glove box. Then he began to walk round the SUV, eyes on the ground, spiraling out and away.

Then he reversed direction and spiraled back. He shut the doors of the SUV.

Not a goddamned thing, Du Pré thought.

He walked out to the main road and back. There had been some traffic on it, several pickups in the last couple of hours.

Du Pré drove on to Cooper and he went to the jail and through the front door and past the dispatcher who hated him to the cells.

Allison Ames was weeping, sitting on the steel bunk. Du Pré took the key from the wall and he opened the cell.

"You don't go to my friend's again," he said. "Maybe you just go on home now. There is nothing here for you."

"Lock the damn door," said Ames. She sniffled and she raised her head.

Du Pré laughed.

"I'm staying," she said. "I am going to get this story."

"That Benson, Drew, him stay," said Du Pré. "Him stay a long time."

"I am not scared," said Allison Ames.

"I am," said Du Pré. He shrugged and he walked out and to his cruiser and he got in, and Allison Ames threw open the other door and she got in, too.

"Please take me back to my car," said Ames. "I promise I won't go back there and go into the cabin."

Du Pré laughed.

Not the same as saying she will not go back there at all.

"It isn't the old man, is it?" she said. "I mean, he wouldn't kill Drew."

"Non," said Du Pré.

"Who is he?" she said.

Du Pré shook his head.

"I don't know," he said. "Miserable old bastard. He is always here, here when my father is here, my grandfather. Benetsee. Him say when he come into the country the Wolf Mountains, they are holes in the ground, grow up since. He watched them."

"That's absurd," said Allison Ames.

Du Pré rolled a smoke and he lit it and Allison Ames rolled down her window and she coughed theatrically for the entire time that Du Pré smoked.

He turned to the road that ran up on the bench and he accelerated until the old cruiser was rasping on the gravel. They crested a hill and Du Pré slowed and he turned to the right and ran along the bench road until he came to the rutted track that led to Benetsee's ramshackle cabin.

There was smoke coming out of the stovepipe.

Pelon was at the woodpile, splitting large wood into stove pieces. He didn't look up when Du Pré drove in.

"He's here," said Allison Ames, and she perked up.

Du Pré sighed.

He stopped the car next to her little white SUV and he shut the engine off. Allison Ames went to her car and she opened the door and got in and looked at her face and she pulled some cosmetics from the glove box.

Benetsee shuffled out on the porch and he sat and looked at Du Pré.

Du Pré got a half gallon of screwtop wine from the trunk of the cruiser and he brought it to the porch and he found a jam jar and he filled it and handed it to the old man, and then he rolled a cigarette and lit it and gave that to him, too.

"You are not so bad a feller," said Benetsee. "That stupid woman, she is in here, yes?"

Du Pré nodded.

"Unhappy woman," said Benetsee, draining the jam jar. Du Pré filled it again.

Allison Ames got out of her SUV.

She squared her shoulders and she marched toward the porch and Du Pré and Benetsee looked at her.

"Mister Benetsay?" she said. "I'm Allison Ames and I am doing a story here, and I would appreciate it very much if you would talk to me."

Benetsee rattled off a speech in Coyote French, and Du Pré listened gravely.

"What did he say?" said Ames.

"Go on home," said Du Pré. "He doesn't want to talk to you. You go in his house, poke around, you got no manners."

Ames flushed.

Benetsee said something else in the Métis patois.

"Well?" said Ames.

"He said what you want is not here anyway, it is in Chicago."

Ames looked stricken.

Benetsee said something else, and a name.

Joe Henderson.

"Jesus," said Ames. She looked shocked.

Pelon came round the corner of the cabin with an armload of stove wood and he went up the steps and inside and they heard the wood fall into the box.

Pelon came back out. He had picked up a small knapsack.

"We go now," he said.

Du Pré nodded.

Benetsee got up and he stepped swiftly off the porch and he landed on the ground and was around the side of the cabin so suddenly it took Ames a moment to grasp that the old man was gone.

She ran to the corner of the cabin and she stopped.

"Where are they?" she said.

She walked back toward the sweat lodge and Du Pré followed.

There was no sign of Benetsee or of Pelon.

The smoke from the stovepipe stopped.

Ames walked back and forth, peering into the trees and looking at the flanks of the mountains.

Two people trotted along a high ridge about three miles up.

"It isn't possible," said Ames.

She turned to Du Pré.

"That can't be them," she said.

Du Pré shrugged.

"It can't be," she said. "No one can run that fast. No one."

Du Pré laughed.

"Go see that Joe Henderson," said Du Pré.

"He couldn't have known about Joe," said Allison Ames.

Du Pré shrugged.

"Him say you are unhappy," said Du Pré.

Allison Ames flushed and she walked away.

Du Pré waited until she drove off.

CHAPTER

29

"They'll find him," said Foote. "Beck is one of their own and they are going to go and get him."

Du Pré waited.

"Du Pré," said Foote, "I would greatly enjoy knowing what you think of all this."

"I don't know," said Du Pré. "There is something I cannot see."

"It doesn't make a lot of sense," said Foote.

"Beck is maybe doing something to make him a lot of money," said Du Pré.

"Why?" said Foote. "He's well paid and he checked out. The man was a high-grade intelligence officer for decades. Nothing untoward on his record. Happily married, three grown children, four grand-kids. Doesn't drink much, smokes a cigar once in a while, exercises regularly. Odenaar Security vets its people carefully, and they follow up on it."

"Yah," said Du Pré. "I got five cards, one don't work, I don't got a flush."

Foote was silent for a while.

"I'll check it," he said.

Du Pré flipped the shoehorn telephone shut and he put it in the glove box in Bart's big dark-green SUV.

Julie was flying in her little aircraft, while Conor and Eamon Burrows stood by the windsock trying not to look worried.

A gust struck the ultralight and Julie sideslipped for a few feet and she leveled it and she dropped down low and followed the little creek. Ducks flew up, quacking indignantly.

She turned the flimsy little plane and she came in and set it down and she zipped along for two hundred feet and then she slowed to a stop. She unbuckled the harness and she got out and took her helmet off and shook her long dark hair out.

She and Conor broke the little plane down. It came apart and folded up to a size small enough to fit in the back of Eamon Burrows's old Volvo.

They all drove down to Raymond and Jacqueline's and there were a couple dozen kids there, some playing on the huge jungle gym that Raymond and Du Pré had built. There were some new parallel bars and a couple of canvas horses and even a set of rings dangling from a crossbar on top of some high poles.

Julie and Conor took two batches of kids and set them to doing stretching exercises. Du Pré went in the house and he got some coffee and he put some bourbon in it and he went to the front steps and he sat, sipping.

He got in his car and drove down to the Toussaint Saloon.

Madelaine was behind the bar, beading something. The tip of her tongue stuck a bit out from the corner of her mouth.

"Fucker," she said, looking at her finger.

"Where is Susan?" said Du Pré.

"School," said Madelaine. "She fill in for somebody sick, not back yet."

Du Pré made himself a ditchwater highball and he sat down on a stool.

"Them people that new roadhouse call, say you are coming this Friday, yes. I say yes. You tell them that you would."

"Shit," said Du Pré. "Me I forgot."

"They didn't," said Madelaine. "Put up posters all over. You look at posters once a while you see there, Du Pré, Bassman, Père Godin play Friday Saturday, that roadhouse."

"Son of a bitch," said Du Pré.

"Good name for a band," said Madelaine. "You ought to think on it."

Bassman came in with Kim. Bassman wasn't wearing a bandage any more but he still had some staples in the skin of his head. He still walked a little slowly.

"We play day after tomorrow," said Du Pré, "that new roadhouse. You are all right?"

"Fuckin' A," said Bassman. "Who is that?"

He went to the door and looked out and then he went out.

"UPS truck," said Madelaine.

Bassman came back with a package the size of a book.

He looked happier.

"Christ," said Du Pré, "they got dogs smell those packages that stuff."

"What stuff?" said Bassman. "It is a book. I join this club. I go read it now, my van, don't have to listen to you." He went out the side door with Kim.

"Maybe it is a book," said Madelaine.

"Yah," said Du Pré. "Bassman, him read a lot."

They both laughed.

"Coyote," said Madelaine.

"Them," said Du Pré. "I tell you bout that old three-toed son of a bitch I hunt two years, him shit on my traps?"

"Yah," said Madelaine, "I know that story. Everybody hunts coyotes has that story, tell."

"I never see the son of a bitch," said Du Pré. "Him get old, I get this call, come out, the road, friend of yours. Him deaf, truck get him one morning early."

"You cry," said Madelaine.

"I tell you this story too many times," said Du Pré.

"You tell that story," said Madelaine, "when you don't got things figured out yet. That is when you tell that story."

Du Pré sipped his drink.

"That Beck," said Du Pré.

Madelaine nodded.

"Maybe," she said, "but where is he?"

Du Pré shook his head.

"Milbank's money," said Du Pré, "it is poison."

"Makes some people ver' crazy," said Madelaine.

Two men came in then, dressed in the worn clothes of longtime bird hunters. They had on scuffed expensive boots. Canvas briefcases.

"Du Pré?" said one.

Du Pré nodded.

"We're from . . . Mr. Fascelli's security company."

Du Pré looked at them.

"Where exactly was Beck's car found?" the same man said.

Du Pré sighed. He filled his glass and he poured it into a plastic go-cup and he went out and got in his cruiser and he drove off, going up to the bench road and along to the cutoff and then the logging road where Beck's red SUV had been found. It sat in the impound lot in Cooper.

Du Pré waited and another of the huge green SUVs Bart liked pulled in beside his old police cruiser. Du Pré got out. He pointed at the spot.

One of the men took out an odd camera, one with a huge lens, and he snapped several photographs. Then they walked on a spiral out from the place. They did not stop and they picked up nothing. They came back.

"Foote said to let you know who we were. There are six of us here. You will probably see only the two of us."

"Got names?" said Du Pré.

"Heubner and Kessel," said the man who had done all the talking.

"I'm Kessel," said the other. He didn't offer his hand.

Du Pré nodded.

"You went over this ground," said Kessel.

Du Pré looked at him.

"Paul Beck didn't just go straight up in the air," said Heubner.

Du Pré looked at him.

"No reason you should trust us," said Kessel.

Du Pré got in his cruiser and he turned it around and he drove off. He passed by Benetsee's on the long way back to Toussaint. There were no signs that anyone had been up the rutted track to the cabin.

Bassman and Kim were in the saloon when Du Pré got back. They were laughing with Madelaine. Du Pré got himself another ditch.

"More help, Du Pré?" said Madelaine.

Du Pré nodded.

"Read your book?" he said to Bassman.

"First chapter," said Bassman. "Very instructive."

Kim looked off, shaking her head.

"You OK to play?" he said.

"Maybe I sit," said Bassman, "I get tired still."

Du Pré nodded.

"You remember that night?" said Du Pré.

Bassman shook his head.

"Fifteen minutes it is just gone," he said. "Don't know anything, time I am walking to the door, go out, and wake up on the stretcher."

Du Pré nodded.

He went out to the front walkway and he looked over at the little airport and the drooping windsock and the Wolf Mountains rising up on the northern horizon.

A small silver plane was droning across the face of the mountains. Some clouds were bunched on the east end, against the highest peaks.

Du Pré rolled a smoke and he sat on a bench. The plane turned and flashed in the sun. Du Pré smoked.

He looked at the dirt of the road. A big black beetle was moving across it. A pickup went past and the beetle dodged out of the way.

Du Pré went back inside.

"Looking for a coyote, Du Pré?" said Madelaine.

Du Pré nodded.

"Truck maybe," he said.

CHAPTER

30

The roadhouse still looked very well kept and new. It had two large pieces of plywood over the holes where the big picture windows had been.

Bassman looked at them and he nodded approvingly.

"Too big," he said. "I never go in them places have these big windows, me I get thrown through them twice."

"Sioux?" said Madelaine.

Bassman nodded.

"It is my fault," he said. "You know how it is, Sioux, me. I say things make them mad."

Du Pré laughed.

Bassman, him, ask some Sioux once they have recipe for Brulé stew. Sioux very sensitive about that. Long time gone, they eat this Jesuit, Father Brulé. Don't like to be reminded of it.

Du Pré and Madelaine and Bassman and Kim went on inside. Carol Canning came bustling over. She looked happy.

"A Billings TV station called and they are going to be here," she said.

"Oh," said Bassman. "Me, I can't play then."

"What you do now?" said Madelaine.

Bassman shrugged.

"North Dakota cop, he—" said Bassman.

"Bassman," said Kim, "doesn't like this cop. The guy lurks behind a highway overpass and busts people for speeding. So he's there and Bassman goes past, doing a hundred and ten, and out he comes. Bassman throws a gallon jug of wine he has open but mostly full out of the window."

"I look in the rearview mirror," said Bassman, "there is all this windshield glass and Gallo, all over the road."

"Cop ends up in the hospital," said Kim. "He's really mad. He gets a judge to sign a warrant."

"Him know where I am," said Bassman, "him be rude."

Du Pré laughed.

"He must have been close," said Madelaine, "hit his windshield with a wine jug."

"Yeah," said Bassman, "him just start to pull around me."

Du Pré roared.

"We get you a false beard," said Madelaine.

"He has no jurisdiction," said Kim. "He can't do anything in Montana."

"Bullshit," said Bassman. "This is *personal.*"

"Put a sack over your head," said Madelaine.

"We've been getting calls all day," said Carol, looking very pleased. "Some people even wanted reserved tables."

"You sell tickets?" said Du Pré.

"First come, first served," said Carol.

"Lots of people coming," said Du Pré. "Local people?"

"They'll be here," said Carol. "But we got calls from as far away as Jackson Hole, Wyoming."

"Oh," said Du Pré.

He looked down at the floor.

"You are not that good," said Madelaine. "Don't you get a fat head, Du Pré."

Du Pré laughed.

They sat for an hour drinking, Du Pré with his ditches and Madelaine with her pink fizzy wine.

A few people from Toussaint came.

More and more people came.

The place was pretty big, and could hold a couple hundred, but they were already here and it was more than an hour before Du Pré and Bassman and Père Godin were supposed to start.

Du Pré went out to check on Bassman, and look for Père Godin's rusty old car.

Bassman and Kim were sitting in Bassman's van in a thick fog of marijuana smoke.

Bassman rolled down the window.

"Maybe we start early," he said. "Lots of people, they just wait, they drink too much maybe."

Du Pré nodded.

"Social conscience," he said, looking at Bassman. "You get beat on the head it improves you."

Bassman nodded.

"I play a lot," he said. "I know crowds."

So did Du Pré. He looked round for Père Godin.

"OK," said Du Pré, "we start then."

Kim kissed Bassman and they got out and they all went in and Du Pré waved to Madelaine who was behind the bar now pulling drinks. It was very busy and people were piled up four deep shouting out orders.

Bassman tuned his bass in two swift twists on the pegs. Du Pré drew the bow over his strings and tightened the A string a little. Then he played a long mournful note, and went into *MacTavish's Reel.*

They played solidly for forty minutes without stopping for applause. Du Pré sang a little, but mostly he played jigs and reels and boatpulling songs. The crowd loved it. They grew silent and then soon there were many couples jammed together on the little dance floor, and still more people coming in.

Père Godin got there and he came up on the stage and he pulled his old accordion from the case and let the bellows fall while he tested notes and Du Pré and Bassman tuned to him and they went on.

The roadhouse was so jammed with people it was impossible to get to the bar or back from it, and people began to pass drinks one way and money the other.

Work this crowd it is hard work, Du Pré thought. He was dripping sweat and had to keep wiping his fingers on a towel and touching the rosin slug.

They played for another hour. It had gotten so hot in the roadhouse from all of the people in it that many of them had gone outside where they could still hear the music and breathe, too.

Du Pré and Bassman slipped out of the side door. The night air felt wonderfully cool.

"Damn," said Bassman, "they like us too much. We got to play bad some, get them crowds down."

He looked around and saw no one coplike, so he lit up a joint.

There were cars and trucks parked all over the lot and even in a pasture across the road, rowed on the grass.

Du Pré looked for Bart and Eamon and Julie and Conor, but he couldn't see Bart's big green SUV or Eamon Burrows's Volvo.

They were probably inside.

Du Pré went to his cruiser and he fished the flask out from under the front seat and he had a couple of swigs and he got the Bull Durham sack from the glove box and he rolled a smoke and he lit it.

"Son of a bitch," said a rancher, "you cain't get that stuff any more."

Du Pré laughed.

"Me, I buy twenty cases," he said. "Got them in the freezer."

"Sell me one?" said the rancher. "The old West died a little more when they quit makin' Bull Durham."

Du Pré went to the trunk and he got a couple of the little sacks for the man.

The rancher offered a ten-dollar bill, but Du Pré waved it away.

A helicopter flew over and circled around a field a half mile away. It set down slowly.

Some flying service.

A van with the logo of the Billings TV station came down the highway, and it slowly passed the roadhouse. When it stopped, two cameramen got out and they put their bulky rigs on their shoulders and walked toward the roadhouse.

"Way too good," said Bassman. "We got to get worse, a hurry. Me, I cannot let them photo my face, there, that North Dakota Highway Patrol him really pissed."

Du Pré laughed.

He saw Bart wandering around in the lot and he walked over.

"Julie, Conor, they are here?" said Du Pré.

"I haven't seen them," said Bart. "We left at the same time and I got here a half hour ago. They were with Eamon in that rustbucket Volvo."

"They got a telephone?" said Du Pré.

"Doesn't work for about thirty miles north of here," said Bart. "Maybe they had a flat. Eamon wanted to talk with the two of them."

Du Pré nodded.

He saw Allison Ames standing near the TV station van, and then she walked round behind it.

"Go look for them," said Du Pré. "Drive back up there. You got them security people here?"

Bart shook his head.

"Two of them were following Eamon Burrows," he said.

"Shit," said Du Pré.

"We got to play, I guess," said Bassman.

"Go see maybe," said Du Pré.

He went back in the roadhouse with Bassman, and they wormed their way up to the stage and got on.

Pere Godin left off talking with the pretty woman he had found and he joined them.

Du Pré started the set with *Baptiste's Lament.*

They played for another hour.

Bassman was looking very tired, and he sat on his amplifier for the second half of the set, but his playing was as good as ever.

Du Pré nodded in time to the music.

He kept looking at the doors far away over the crowd for Bart.

But he did not come.

The set ended and they went out again, along with almost everyone else. The air in the roadhouse was stifling.

Du Pré saw Bart's big green SUV pull up. There was no place to park. Bart waved at Du Pré.

Du Pré walked over.

"You were right," said Bart. "They disappeared. I found the two security men. They were following a mile or so behind, had a flat."

Du Pré nodded.

"Somebody threw a nail strip over the road," said Bart.

"Shit," said Du Pré.

CHAPTER

31

"Christ, I blew it," said Bart. His face was red and angry.

"*Non*," said Madelaine, "you all think that it is safe."

"Think," said Bart. He looked at the shoehorn telephone and he picked it up and took it outside and Madelaine and Du Pré and Bassman and Kim glanced at each other and shrugged.

Bassman yawned and sagged.

"I got to sleep," he said. "Go to the van maybe."

Kim led him out the side door.

Carol Canning brought a paper sack to Du Pré. He handed it to Madelaine.

"Almost a thousand," Carol said. "We did real good." She yawned. The place was lit up and her husband was mopping the floor. All of the chairs had been set up on the tables.

Madelaine counted the money, fifties and twenties and tens and fives. She swiftly made three piles. Père Godin took his and he went out the door.

"Thank you, Père," said Du Pré.

The old man waved once and he was gone.

"Him got a grass widow out there," said Madelaine. "Wonder if some husband shoot him sometime."

Du Pré laughed.

Bart came back in. He handed the phone to Du Pré.

"Yah," said Du Pré.

"Something very bad is going on there," said Foote. "I'm sending more people. None of this makes sense yet."

"No," said Du Pré. "But maybe it will."

"And?" said Foote.

"Don't know," said Du Pré.

"Just a minute," said Foote. He rang off. Du Pré rolled a smoke and he lit it and he waited.

"They found Beck's body," said Foote, "at Stinking Water Creek."

"Shit," said Du Pré.

"Will you . . . ?" said Foote.

"Yah," said Du Pré. He shut the telephone up.

"They find Beck's body," said Du Pré to Bart. Bart nodded.

"Well," said Bart, "at least it isn't him."

"I am going there," said Du Pré. "You take Madelaine home, yes?"

Du Pré kissed Madelaine.

"Watch your ass," said Madelaine. "Me, I watch his. Kim, she drive Bassman. We are all right."

"You don't stop," said Du Pré.

Madelaine shook her head.

They went out and Bart got in the passenger side of his big green SUV. Madelaine stood there, looking at Du Pré.

"What you think, Du Pré?" she said.

Du Pré shook his head.

He looked at the trucks and cars left in the pasture and the lot. There were still dozens of them. Lots of people had gone to sleep in their vehicles rather than drive drunk.

Du Pré saw Allison Ames get out of her little white SUV. She looked at him, and she waved her arms.

"Jesus," said Du Pré.

Madelaine shrugged.

Du Pré walked over the the journalist.

She was shaking. She opened the door of the SUV and she pointed to the screen of her computer.

A picture of three people, bound with duct tape.

Eamon, Conor, and Julie.

TELL DU PRE THANKS FOR MAKING IT SO EASY. WE WILL BE IN TOUCH.

"Son of a bitch!" said Du Pré. "You get this when?"

"Two minutes ago," said Ames. "It beeps when there is an urgent message. Jesus, Du Pré, what is going on?"

Du Pré looked at her.

"How they do this?" he said.

"If they have the codes," said Ames, "they can do this. The computer runs off satellites."

"Shit," said Du Pré.

"What is going on?" said Ames. "Is this a kidnapping?"

Du Pré turned and walked away. He went to the big SUV and he rapped on the window. Bart opened it, looking distraught.

"Get Foote," said Du Pré.

Bart dialed and he handed the shoehorn phone to Du Pré.

"Yes?" said Foote.

"Somebody get Julie, the Burrows," said Du Pré. "I am so smart I think it OK they go, Cannings' roadhouse. They thank me for making it easy."

"Jesus," said Foote, "Whoever these people are, they know all the dodges."

"You are sure it is not these security people, Bart's?" said Du Pré.

"Beck is dead," said Foote. "He can't spend much money that way."

"So who is this?" said Du Pré.

"I could hazard a guess," said Foote, "given what little we know. The most logical explanation is that it is Milbank's people. He has his toadies around him, they have a lot of petty cash, perhaps they began to dig for the Lewis and Clark stuff and then decided that with all that money offered, they would get it."

"Why take Julie, the Burrows?" said Du Pré.

"Pressure Bart to pressure Milbank," said Foote. "These bastards are good, I will give them that."

"They send me message, Allison Ames computer," said Du Pré.

"Very good indeed," said Foote. "Somebody was there tonight."

"Hundreds of people here tonight," said Du Pré.

"Let me talk to Bart," said Foote.

Du Pré sighed and he handed the telephone to Bart, who looked puzzled. Then he listened for a minute and he glared at Du Pré. He said a few words and he shut the telephone up.

"Thanks," said Bart, "you son of a bitch."

"I was going to tell you," said Du Pré, "when we got back."

"You fucker," said Bart. "What did you think I would do?"

"Call Foote," said Du Pré, "we maybe find something out."

Bart nodded.

"The phone," he said.

"Yah," said Du Pré, "but they are there long time before we are. I am some stupid."

Bart sighed.

"So," he said, "now what?"

"They will call back," said Du Pré.

"We should call the FBI," said Bart.

"Morning maybe," said Du Pré. "All we know they are in on this."

Bart laughed.

"It was J. Edgar Hoover on the grassy knoll," he said.

Du Pré shrugged.

Allison Ames had followed him.

"Look," she said, "I am in this now and I really do not like it, at all. This is frightening."

Du Pré looked at her.

"You lie some," he said.

Ames looked bewildered.

"Money," said Du Pré, "for money."

Ames looked puzzled.

"All I want," she said, "is a goddamned book. A good article."

"They use you," said Du Pré.

"Like that?" said Ames, gesturing toward her SUV. "Yeah they do. But if you think I have fuck-all to do with a kidnapping . . ."

She threw up her hands and she walked away.

"She is telling the truth maybe," said Madelaine.

Du Pré snorted.

"What?" said Madelaine.

"They play her," said Du Pré. "She is stupid. They give her information, she thinks it is for her. It is not, it is for what she will do."

"They kill her," said Madelaine.

Du Pré nodded.

"Shit, Du Pré," said Madelaine. "What are these people."

Du Pré shook his head.

Bassman's van pulled up and Kim shut it off and turned off the headlights and she got out.

"He's flat out," she said, "poor baby. He worked himself to death tonight."

"So what we do, Du Pré?" said Madelaine.

"Go home," said Du Pré. "They got what they need now don't need more."

Madelaine nodded.

Bart was sitting in his seat, his face in his hands.

Du Pré went to the window.

"I am sorry," he said.

Bart nodded.

"I can't act," he said. "You did the right thing."

Du Pré put his hand on Bart's shoulder and Bart grabbed it and pressed it.

"Thanks," said Bart.

"Yah," said Du Pré.

"Who killed Beck?" said Bart. "Why, for God's sake?"

Du Pré shrugged.

Madelaine got in the driver's side and she started the big SUV.

"Don't stop," said Du Pré.

Madelaine nodded.

"You be home tomorrow?" she said.

"Think so," said Du Pré.

"Go now then," said Madelaine. "Don't have to pass us then."

Du Pré got in his old cruiser.

He started it and he wheeled out of the parking lot.

Three minutes later he was on the highway north, and the cruiser was getting up to speed.

CHAPTER

32

"State boys are on the way," said Highway Patrolman McPhie.

Du Pré nodded. He walked carefully around Beck's body. Beck was on his back, arms flung out. His face was gone, chewed off by skunks and badgers and coyotes. His teeth were broken. A dark stain of blood spread out from under Beck's head.

A shiny stainless steel 9mm Sig Sauer pistol was three feet from Beck's right hand.

"They get pissy we tromp around much," said McPhie. "You want my opinion, he was murdered and they wanted it taken fer suicide. Feller shoots himself in the mouth, the barrel's inside and his teeth stay where God put 'em."

Du Pré nodded.

The light was coming up and it slanted well. Du Pré squatted on his haunches and he looked carefully at the ground.

"He was blindfolded probably," said McPhie. "Shot him in the mouth, took the tape off his wrists. They've been chewed a little but there's a couple pieces of gum on 'em. Moved him a little . . ."

Du Pré nodded.

"What the hell is this about?" said McPhie. "Not that I like pryin' . . ."

Du Pré shook his head.

"Money," he said.

"Oh," said McPhie, "that."

Du Pré stood up.

"Kid found him," said McPhie. "Lookin' for a lost horse. This little patch can't be seen from the road, but, hell, it ain't a hundred feet in . . ."

Du Pré looked back at the county road. Beck's SUV had been found a half mile away. Should have used dogs, he thought. God damn it.

Du Pré looked over at the Odenaar Security men. They were leaning against their car. It had several aerials on it.

"If I liked 'em better," said McPhie, "I'd a let 'em come close fer a look, but I just don't like 'em."

Du Pré laughed.

"Been dead maybe four, five days," said McPhie.

Du Pré nodded.

"They killed him right away," he said.

"What is this about?" said McPhie.

"I don't know yet," said Du Pré. He walked toward the two security men.

"Well," said one.

"He was murdered," said Du Pré.

The two men nodded. They got in their rig and they drove off.

Flashing lights danced across the tree trunks. The State of Montana criminalists had arrived.

They parked their van a good fifty feet from any other vehicle. They put on moon suits and they picked up heavy packs and clumped back toward McPhie, running into tree trunks every once in a while. Their face masks were not well designed.

McPhie backed away.

The technicians knelt by Beck's body. They opened cases and they began to take samples and one of them took photographs of the body. Another looked very closely at the ground.

They scraped under Beck's fingernails and they took several close-ups of Beck's mouth and his shattered teeth. They filled more glassine envelopes with this and that.

Then they got up and took off the moon suits.

"Won't tell us *shit!*" said one.

Another van pulled up and two men got out with dispatch. They went to the rear of the van and opened it and pulled out a gurney and they carried it through the trees back to Beck's body. They pulled on rubber gloves and they lifted Beck up and put him in a black body bag and they put the bag on the gurney and they picked it up like a stretcher and all four of them carried the body to the second van and they put it inside and shut the doors and the two men got back in and drove away.

The criminalists all lit cigarettes. They sucked in the smoke and blew it out their nostrils.

Du Pré walked over.

"It wasn't a suicide," said one.

Du Pré nodded.

"He was blindfolded and taped," said a second. "If he'd done it his teeth would not have been shot away."

Du Pré nodded.

"What is this about?" said another.

Du Pré shook his head. He walked away and then back to the trees to McPhie, who was standing near his patrol cruiser.

"Gabriel," said McPhie, "you ain't in too deep now are you?"

Du Pré laughed.

"Thought I'd ask," said McPhie. "You know, since these rich bastards started comin' round things have got wild and woolly. I recall it was danged peaceful here once upon a time. This got anything to do with those things you found, the Lewis and Clark stuff?"

Du Pré shrugged.

"Maybe," he said. "But I think it is about money now. Somebody sees a chance to get a lot of it."

McPhie nodded.

"Feds be in on it?" he said.

Du Pré shrugged.

161

"Probably," he said. "Benny he can ask, or the state can ask. They will do an autopsy, they won't find anything. Beck was killed with that one shot. Killed here."

McPhie nodded.

"I can't track so good," he said, "but you could see where he walked in?"

"Him, one other person," said Du Pré. "Beck behind. Maybe got a rope on his hands, he is pulled along. Take him there, take the tape off his mouth, try to shoot him when his mouth is open."

"They are bastards," said McPhie.

"Him hit Beck a couple times," said Du Pré. "Maybe saying, 'Open your mouth,' and he will not so shoot him through his teeth."

"Somebody was coming by," said McPhie.

Du Pré nodded.

"One man?" said McPhie.

Du Pré nodded.

McPhie shook his head.

"How you do that?" he said. "Tell from the ground. I mean, I can see a *footprint*."

"Got to lift the ground up to your eyes," said Du Pré. "Catfoot he say that, over and over. Got to lift the ground up to your eyes."

"Catfoot," said McPhie. "I only met him the once when I was a kid. Hell of a feller."

Du Pré laughed.

"He was that," said Du Pré.

Catfoot in his moccasins and old hat so worn it dripped down his head and his pants with the buckskin seat. Cloth wore out on the saddle.

The state vans left.

"Wonder what they'll find," said McPhie.

"Nothing," said Du Pré.

"There are two others drove with them," said Du Pré. "Come on, I show you."

He led McPhie slowly back toward the road. Du Pré pointed to a spot on a skinny pine, dead. McPhie squinted at it.

"Little pieces of bar broke off there," he said.

"Man stumble," said Du Pré, "grab that. See?"

He pointed to the ground. A thick branch was buried in the needles and duff. One end was clear of fallen stuff.

"Stumbled on that," said McPhie.

Du Pré went on to the road. He turned right and he walked down about fifteen feet.

Three cigarette butts sat together on the ground, just off the graded part of the road.

"They were in the car here," said McPhie.

Du Pré nodded.

"Three together, maybe twenty minutes, half hour, this person is some nervous," he said.

McPhie looked off into the woods.

"They stay in the car?" he said.

"This one did," said Du Pré. "Other man walked around front, moved there to see better."

"Three of them and Beck," said McPhie.

Du Pré nodded.

"Twenty minutes is a long time," said McPhie. "They must have wanted something from Beck."

Du Pré nodded.

"What do you think?" said McPhie.

"Something that they wanted to know," said Du Pré. "Beck, he knew he was going to die. He probably told them something, maybe they could check, it was not right, so . . . maybe codes for computer or something like that."

McPhie nodded.

"I appreciate the instruction," he said. "I really do."

Du Pré looked off into the woods.

"Go up there," he said. "Wait. There will be a small white SUV coming here, any time now. Woman driving it is Allison Ames."

"Who's she?" said McPhie.

"Journalist," said Du Pré.

"Why is she coming here?" said McPhie.

"Somebody tell her to," said Du Pré. "On the computer."

"Shit," said McPhie. "Then they aren't that good."

"*Non,*" said Du Pré. "They are not."

CHAPTER

33

"I can't fucking believe this," said Markham Milbank. "In this world? I can't believe it."

He was standing on the porch of the Toussaint Saloon, hands in his pockets. He trembled.

"I get told that if I send a whole lot of money to Macao where it will be for maybe thirty seconds before going off someplace else that your people will be released and I will get the Lewis and Clark stuff. Which I don't even want anymore. It was a game and it isn't fun any more. No fun at all. Who are these bastards anyway?"

Bart looked at him.

"It is what happens," he said, "When you screw around. Past the first couple of million, which you can grasp, it is just funny numbers. They don't mean anything anymore. But it means a hell of a lot to some people. Hell, people get murdered every day for what is in their wallets, and no one carries much cash anymore."

"God," said Milbank, "I'll pay 'em the money. I don't care about the money. But how do we know they will let them go? Shouldn't the FBI come in on this? They do kidnappings, don't they?"

"Paul Beck was killed," said Bart. "And Paul Beck isn't easy to kill."

Milbank looked up the street. The weird motor home with the satellite dishes on the roof was lumbering toward the saloon.

He had driven alone in a rented Cadillac.

Du Pré sat on the edge of the boardwalk, smoking.

"So what do you want me to do?" he said.

Bart looked at Du Pré.

"Those two you had with you, vice presidents or something?" said Du Pré.

"Pat Henkel and Jerry Soldner," said Milbank. "Been with me since the beginning. They took off last night. Some fuss at the plant."

"You got a telephone?" said Du Pré.

"Yeah," said Milbank, looking puzzled.

"They are not there," said Du Pré. "So you call and find that out maybe."

Milbank turned pale.

"Oh, God," he said. "Not them. Jesus, they don't need the money."

Du Pré shrugged.

Milbank ran to the motor home and he went in and he was back in two minutes.

"You were right," he said. "They never came and there was no emergency. I can't believe it. They were my *friends*."

"What you will find, I expect," said Bart, "is that they lost a lot of money someplace. The stock market. Some spec venture that took a lot of capital."

"These days," said Milbank, "that's easy enough."

"Where is your security guy?" said Du Pré.

"Torbert? He went off a couple of days ago to check something or other out. Jesus Christ, you're not serious," said Milbank.

"Oh, but we are," said Bart, "and it seems your nearest and dearest are in this together. Torbert killed Paul Beck, I think. Beck was smart, way too smart for anyone but an old buddy. Beck was a brave man, and he wouldn't make it easy for them."

"Jesus," said Milbank, "what do I do?"

Du Pré put his butt on the ground and he stepped on it and he came back up on the porch.

"You don't send the money quick," he said. "You delay. They are not all that far from here, maybe Billings, maybe someplace closer. Your . . . Soldner and Henkel they are out of the country, they are waiting for the money, someplace. But that Thommassen is here. He has Julie, the Burrows."

"God!" said Milbank. "I'll—"

"Do what?" said Bart. "Fire them?"

"Jesus," said Milbank, "the money started coming in in a flood and then a tidal wave and I had no idea."

A window opened in the motor home and an arm stuck out and waved.

Milbank ran to the door and he went in.

"That little shit," said Bart.

"Him don't mean no harm," said Du Pré. "He is not greedy. So he don't think anyone else is either."

"He pisses me off," said Bart. "In case you forgot, my niece is out there someplace and she may be dead."

Du Pré shook his head.

"Non," he said. "They kill one man, that is bad enough, they kill Julie, the Burrows, you are after them forever, they know that."

"Goddamned right," said Bart.

"They are going to screw Thommassen, too, let him pay for Beck," said Du Pré. "Thommassen he is smart, he will expect that. So we have that trouble there."

"Henkel and Soldner won't play for keeps," said Bart.

Du Pré shook his head.

Milbank came back.

"You were right," he said. "I told them I had to get some liquidity. They understand that."

Bart's shoehorn telephone rang and he opened it and clapped it to his ear and he walked away, listening. He said something and he shut the telephone back up.

"That was Foote," he said. "If your two clowns left the country, they did it in the dark. Their passports haven't been used. No airline has them on a manifest."

"Private plane?" said Milbank.

Bart shook his head.

"Harder than you think," he said. "What with the military these days, they keep a close eye on all flights. Since the unpleasantness in New York and Washington."

Du Pré wandered into the saloon. It had just opened and Madelaine had the television on. There had been a bad accident near Billings. An SUV, now in flames. The fire department was there. So was a crew in a helicopter. Du Pré watched the fire trucks shoot foam on the blazing SUV.

A reporter on the ground said it was a single-vehicle accident and there were no witnesses.

A fireman said they didn't know how many people were in the SUV.

". . . back to you, Cicely . . ." said the reporter.

The camera focused again on the SUV. It was sitting upright in the barrow pit. Du Pré studied the picture.

He made himself a ditchwater highball and he carried it back outside.

He nodded to Bart. They walked away from Milbank, who was hopping up and down a little where he stood.

"Those guys, Milbank's," said Du Pré, "they are dead now maybe. There is this accident near Billings, show the SUV, but it did not roll over. Roof is fine and there are no marks. Just tracks down into the pit."

"Shit," said Bart. "You want to call your FBI guy?"

Du Pré stood silent for a moment.

"No," he said. "It is that Thommassen, him, who he got with him now. They are pret' smart. FBI comes in, they know it, maybe they just run."

"And leave no witnesses," said Bart.

Du Pré nodded.

"You sure about those idiots of Milbank's?" said Bart.

Du Pré shrugged.

"How many SUVs we got here just burst into flames?" he said. "They roll over. They are designed to do that. Good thing, too."

"But we don't know," said Bart.

Du Pré shrugged.

"This guy Thommassen," said Du Pré. "He worked for who? CIA maybe? This is his one big chance. He won't take any risks with it. They are dead, you bet, they aren't worth anything to him any more."

Milbank went back to the odd motor home.

"Hey, Du Pré," said Madelaine. "Two bodies in that SUV, pret' bad burned. News says they are in the back seat, though. Cops, they are looking for the driver."

"Did we bet?" said Bart. "I would like to give you five bucks anyway."

Du Pré snorted.

"Du Pré," said Madelaine, "you got breakfast here now. You, too, Bart."

They went in to their platters of bacon and eggs and hashbrowns and biscuits.

The news was about baseball scores, and then some young man with a neck wider than his head grunted something when asked questions.

Milbank came in.

"Well," he said, "it is one of our best and most secure systems. The Department of Defense uses it to protect vital information."

"How good?" said Bart.

"Anything can be broken, usually," said Milbank, "but not this one. It has five sets of random interlocks. The math is impossible."

"Nothing," said Bart, "is impossible."

"This truly is," said Milbank. "It runs all round the world before it comes in. We can't even do an interval grab on it. It is too fast and too random. No, this is the system that made my money. It is good. Too good."

"Your vice presidents," said Bart. "Got burned up in an SUV in Billings. We think."

"Jesus," said Milbank.

"Thought you'd like to know," said Bart.

"Are you sure?" said Milbank.

Bart shrugged.

The news went back to the accident. Firemen and cops were peering in the holes where the glass had been in the SUV. A door was pried open. Something very black was pulled out.

Milbank was chewing with nothing in his mouth.

"God," he said.

"If this works out all right," said Bart, "I'm only going to break your jaw."

Milbank blinked.

"Jesus," he said, "I meant no harm."

Bart drank coffee.

"Then why," he said, "are all of these people dead?"

CHAPTER

34

"Wonders of modern times, man," said Harvey Wallace, Blackfeet and FBI. "Here's what we got on Torbert Thommassen. Classified. Classified. Big glop of Magic Marker. Classified. Classified. Well, he was born 9.17.1943. Wesleyan. After college, and this is just my guess after years of looking at this crap, good old Torbert was out there in badland smiting Commies. He seems to have been very good at his job. I can tell because even though I have a very high security rating, I still don't get dick, but I do get a lot of Magic Marker. What you got here is one AAA spook. Frankly, these guys scare me."

"How's your wife?" said Du Pré.

"She scares me more'n he does. Now, the question is, do you want our help. And my answer is no. You do not want our help. Thing about our help is we have all these procedures and such shit, and once they are set in train they run on and you get Waco. Ruby Ridge. This wouldn't come to my desk now, anyway. I got promoted. I have nice crimes now. Serial killers, child murderers, that sort of stuff. I don't do kidnappings. No, my friend, if he is there and you are there, then you have a much better chance of getting those people back alive."

"So," said Du Pré, "some dumbass asks you for help you will say no."

"Bart?" said Harvey.

"No comment," said Du Pré. "You got any suggestions?"

"Nothing you wouldn't have thought of. One, demand proof that they are still alive. Don't buy newspapers, they are hours old. Demand that the three of them be exhibited in good health in front of the tube. CNN is a good backdrop. Up to the minute. Another thing about Thommassen. He will not panic, which is good. He does not care, I would think, to kill Julie Perelli and the Burrows. It is wasteful and in poor taste. He won't blow a gasket and kill them in a frenzy. So don't screw it up, and I expect they will be fine."

"Yah," said Du Pré.

"Once the money is transferred," said Harvey, "Torbert will want proof. Once he has the proof, then he just has to get someplace where he can get at his money. Stick his electronic fingers in the pile. So it isn't like he has to pick up a suitcase or otherwise expose himself, and I would think he has several routes out of the country planned. He will keep it very simple, Du Pré. Simple and easy to back out of. You will not be pounding across the prairie on your hoss after him, hoping to catch him before he makes it to the border. He can wait a long time before he slips away. He's really smart."

"Yah," said Du Pré, "and I am not so smart maybe."

"Oh," said Harvey, "you were clever enough to call me."

"Shit," said Du Pré.

"A thought," said Harvey. "Torbert there is a very smart spook and when you complicate things, of course, the odds that something will go wrong increase. It is hard to move three people around who you have captive. If you have help it is hard, and Torbert will probably want to keep his labor costs down. Or the number of people he has to kill. You said that two of that ass Milbank's employees were betoasted in an SUV?"

"They maybe started all of this," said Du Pré.

"He'll have one other person out there," said Harvey. "Torbert is with his chips. But there is another thing. The person he has eyeballing you all may well not know he's working for Torbert. Old spook habit. Find a fucking fool to take the pie in the face."

"Jesus," said Du Pré, "that reporter, that Allison Ames."

"You would know better than I," said Harvey, "and now I must return to the matter of the swine in Phoenix who is dismembering prostitutes with surgical knives. As if those poor women don't have enough trouble already."

"Good hunting," said Du Pré.

"Love to Madelaine," said Harvey. "Don't call back, at least not about your goddamned kidnapping."

"What?" said Bart.

"He say no, we don't want them," said Du Pré. "Where is that Milbank?"

"Out in his electronic playland," said Bart, "awaiting word from whoever has Julie and the Burrows."

They walked to the huge motor home and Du Pré banged on the door and a flunk came and opened it. They went in.

Markham Milbank was seated before a huge television screen. He had a computer console in front of him, a little thing the size of a thin briefcase.

The screen was blue.

Then it flickered, and a live image showed.

Julie Perelli. Her hands were taped and she had transparent tape over her mouth. CNN News was going on on a screen behind her. Milbank looked at a small television and he nodded.

"Real time," he said. "She's there and she's alive."

A hand reached out and jerked the tape from Julie's mouth.

"Uncle Bart," she said, "we are OK. Conor and Mister Burrows are fine. It is eleven twenty-one on Thursday—" The image went away. Letters appeared on the screen.

Account and routing numbers and a time runoff.

Milbank tapped in a message.

The time runout added sixty minutes.

"He just gave us an hour," said Milbank. "So what do we do?"

Du Pré looked at Bart.

"Send it," said Bart. He was writing down the account and routing numbers.

Milbank watched him.

"It won't do much good," he said, pointing to the screen. "See?"

Ct #'s invalid check 1245 hours.

"I have to have the bank ready," said Milbank. "He'll give us perhaps three minutes to do the transaction. It will go wherever, and be sent out of there and out of wherever is next. It takes a good hour to track a single set of numbers. So with each step he multiples his lead by sixty. Shit, he could have it back here before we plodded through Luxembourg."

"Those were phony numbers," said Bart.

"Yup," said Milbank. "If I'd bitten and sent 'em the money, the bank wouldn't have accepted electronic delivery of it. He's good. Wants to see how fast we are."

"He knows," said Bart.

"So . . . ," said Milbank.

Ninety minutes, thought Du Pré.

He went outside to his cruiser and he put his hands on the top and he looked up at the Wolf Mountains. They were cut by clouds, and the white peaks floated in the sky.

Du Pré looked to his right.

Allison Ames's little white SUV sat there.

She was in it, looking down at something in her lap.

Du Pré walked over the gravel to the little white four-wheel car.

She still didn't notice him.

He jerked the door open.

"Jesus!" she screamed, looking up from the laptop computer.

"What are you doing?" he said.

"My fucking job," she said.

"The Lewis and Clark stuff?" said Du Pré. "You want it?"

"That's why I came," she said.

"It is in the bar there, the cooler, a banana box," said Du Pré. "Here, I get it for you."

He went in and got the box with the lettuce on top of the journal and the artifacts. He carried it back out to Allison Ames's white SUV. He set it on the hood.

Allison Ames got out of the car and she went very slowly to the box. She lifted the flaps and she peered in. She picked up the oilcloth-wrapped journal, the sextant and the bullet mold, and she touched the lead canister of gunpowder.

"It is theirs, isn't it?" she said.

173

"Yah," said Du Pré, "it is theirs."

"I thought the old man had it," she said. "Benett, Benee."

"Benetsee," said Du Pré, "him give them to me."

"They were here all along," said Allison Ames.

"Yah," said Du Pré.

"It was true," she said.

Du Pré nodded.

"What if I just take them?" she said.

Du Pré shrugged.

Allison Ames put the box in the back of her SUV and she got in.

"Why are you giving them to me?" she said.

"I am not," said Du Pré. "You are taking them."

"You could stop me," she said.

"Don't have to," said Du Pré. "You think about what you will do with them?"

"Get them into a vault," she said.

"You drive off with them," said Du Pré, "you don't make it very far."

Ames looked at him.

"The old man," she said, "he does magic. I don't think so."

Du Pré laughed.

She got back out of the SUV.

"What is the catch?" she said. "What is it? I can take them to Billings and hand them over to the government."

Du Pré nodded.

Her computer began to beep.

Ames ignored it.

She sighed and she got the box and she gave it back to Du Pré.

"What do you want?" she said.

"Who is on your computer?" said Du Pré.

"An archivist," said Allison Ames. "I write my stuff down and send it off so there is a record. It gets done instantly."

Du Pré nodded.

"Do this for a long time?" he said.

"No," she said, "I got a good deal. New company. Really cheap compared to the others. Really cheap."

"This company," said Du Pré, "it is in Texas maybe?"

"Yeah," said Ames, "how did you know?"

CHAPTER

35

Du Pré left Ames with Markham Milbank.

He put the banana crate back in the cooler.

Bart was sitting at the bar drinking club soda and lime.

"Do you know what is going on?" he said.

Du Pré shook his head.

"Du Pré," said Madelaine, putting a ditch down in front of him, "how you like this? Computers? I get you one, your birthday."

"I shoot myself now," said Du Pré, "save me the trouble, you the money."

"Computers are fine things," said Bart. "Unfortunately people haven't changed much. My grandfather tied business competitors to old jukeboxes or concrete blocks and sent them to the bottom of Lake Michigan. My father had his shot. I just mug them financially. I don't even do it. I pay people to do that."

"Your grandfather, father," said Madelaine, "probably they pay people do the jukeboxes, fire the guns."

"Indeed," said Bart, "they did."

"So," said Madelaine, "what now?"

"That little prick," said Bart, "is going to send the money. I am going to see he does that, and I am gonna see my niece again."

The telephone rang. Madelaine picked up the receiver.

"Bart," she said, "it is Julie's mother."

Bart winced and he went to the telephone.

"Don't tell her anything," said Madelaine, hand over the mouthpiece.

Bart took the phone and he went back in the hallway.

"So," said Madelaine, "this Allison Ames, she is not part of this?"

"She don't know she is," said Du Pré. "Does now. They are better than I thought."

"What you think, Du Pré?" she said.

Du Pré shrugged.

"Send the money," he said, "then they will move I think. They are not far away. Billings probably. That Thommassen he is smart. Too smart to try to hide in the country. Lots of old buildings in Billings. Lots of places, people go in and out of. Nobody thinks about it."

Benny Klein rushed in, face flushed, waving a sheet of paper.

"Du Pré," he said, "lookit this."

He handed it to Du Pré.

Du Pré read it.

"Guy was in the jail there," said Benny, "said a couple other guys talked about beating up a Indian and a girl in the parking lot of a roadhouse. They were paid to do it by somebody they never saw. Couple grand apiece . . ."

"They are there?" said Du Pré.

"Not any more," said Benny. "I was talking to a cop down there, happened to know about this, wondered about which roadhouse."

Du Pré nodded.

"When they get out, them two?" he said.

"Yesterday morning," said Benny. "They were in on some misdemeanor, got in a fight I think."

Du Pré got up and he rubbed the back of his neck.

Bart was talking in soothing tones.

Du Pré looked at the sheet.

"We get pictures maybe of these guys?" he said.

Benny looked crestfallen.

"I shoulda thought of that," he said. "I'll go and see." He ran out and his car roared off.

Du Pré drummed his fingers on the bartop.

"Make a mistake?" said Madelaine.

Du Pré nodded.

"Bad one?" she said.

"Julie, the Burrows," he said, "no mistake is good."

She put her hand on his.

"Find that coyote," she said.

Du Pré nodded.

"I think maybe that Thommassen kills those two, Milbank's people. Now I think maybe not. Maybe the two, the SUV that burned, are those guys. Ones Benny was talking about."

"He don't talk to me," said Madelaine.

"Guy in jail, Billings, says two guys there talked, beating up an Indian, a girl, roadhouse, paid good for it. They get out yesterday morning, maybe they go, get the rest of their money."

"He is too smart let them know where he is," said Madelaine.

"He find them, say, come on, I give you a ride to the money," said Du Pré. "Those two dickheads, Milbank's, they are still alive then."

"So?" said Madelaine.

"They are not so stupid after all," said Du Pré. "I am stupid. God damn that Benetsee."

"What him do?" said Madelaine.

Du Pré shook his head.

"I don't know," he said, "but he did it. I know that. Old son of a bitch."

Madelaine put her hands in the air.

"You, ditch," she said, making him another. "You get like this, chew on your own leg, me, I got to listen to the whining."

Du Pré laughed.

Markham Milbank came running in, face alight.

"If the information is correct," he said, "Ames' stuff went to Texas. A blind box. But it has been used in the last hour."

"Blind box?" said Du Pré.

"Somebody looked at the information," said Milbank, "is all. But that means that they wanted it."

Bart came back from the hall. He put the phone back on the cradle and he sighed.

"I just lied to my sister," he said.

Madelaine laughed.

Bart looked at Milbank.

"You," he said, "are going to send that money."

Milbank nodded.

He looked at his watch.

"In seventeen minutes," he said.

They went out to the motor home and sat in front of the big computer screen. It had a picture of snowy mountains on it. Clouds moved over their peaks.

Du Pré went outside to smoke.

He looked at the dirt.

He nodded.

He had his cigarette, and he went to his cruiser and got the flask from under the front seat and he had a swallow and he put it back.

He looked at the line of willows that banked the little creek. A bird flashed as it flew, blue iridescence.

Kingfisher.

This I understand, but what there is in that motor home I do not understand, Du Pré thought, but people they do not change.

How did this start?

He shook his head.

He rolled another smoke.

He looked up at the Wolf Mountains.

He snorted and he walked back toward the saloon and up on the board porch and he sat on the bench he had built long ago.

Julie, the Burrows, they maybe live, they maybe don't.

No reason to kill them but there was no reason for any of this.

Money.

Madelaine came out with a ditch in one hand and a glass of pink wine in the other. She sat down.

"Susan is there now," said Madelaine. "You are here, thinking about that coyote?"

Du Pré nodded.

"Pret' smart, coyote," said Madelaine.

Du Pré laughed.

God's Dog.

A joker, a thief, a scoundrel.

"You like them coyotes," said Madelaine.

"This one, I don't like," said Du Pré.

"All that crap," said Madelaine, waving her hand at the motor home and the dish antennas, "all that crap and they are not happy. Are you happy, Du Pré?"

"I get Julie, the Borrows back, I am happy," said Du Pré. "She is a good kid. Too much money. Her mother won't spend money, it does not help."

"Why they don't ask Bart?" said Madelaine. "He is her uncle."

Du Pré nodded.

"So they want, hurt this Milbank," said Madelaine.

Du Pré nodded.

"Also Bart is tougher," said Madelaine. "He is getting better, he don't even get drunk this time."

Du Pré laughed.

"This is all over," he said, "Bart get drunk. I get drunk with him."

"Maybe," said Madelaine. "It is better long time gone. We fight over buffalo then."

"Die maybe twenty-five," said Du Pré, "starve every winter, one kid out of five maybe lives, eighteen, no, it was not better."

"It will be all right," said Madelaine. "Benetsee, he don't tell you things, they don't come true."

"He don't tell me nothing this time," said Du Pré.

Madelaine looked at him.

"Think, Du Pré," she said.

Du Pré rolled a smoke and he lit it and gave it to her. She took a long drag and handed it back.

"I don't know," said Du Pré.

"Think," said Madelaine.

Bart came out of the motor home.

"He sent the money," said Bart.

Du Pré stood up.

"Billings," he said. "We go there now."

CHAPTER

36

"Not as good as your old boat, is it?" said Bart. He glanced over at Du Pré. A security agent named Bollard was in the back, staring at a computer screen.

I don't even want to know, Du Pré thought.

"Why do you think they are there?" said Bart.

"It is the biggest city in Montana," said Du Pré. "Lots of shipping, oil refineries, trains, plenty of places to hide. Rest of Montana, it is not so easy to hide. Lots of ways to get out of it, I think that is what Thommassen will do."

"And the last message from him said directions to Julie and the Burrows would arrive in six hours," said Bart. "Which gives him a lot of time."

"He won't be leaving from the airport," said Bollard, "and the cops are going to be watching the bus station. I doubt he'll be going Greyhound."

"Milbank just sent off forty million without a squawk," said Bart. "I am trying not to hate him so much."

Du Pré laughed.

They were well past the Missouri headed south. Bart was going about eighty in the huge green SUV. It began to shimmy if he went faster.

"It's a big place," said Bart.

Du Pré nodded and he watched the green on the plains. There had been a lot of rain, for Montana.

They were silent for an hour.

"Oh my God," said Bollard.

Du Pré looked at him.

"Son of a bitch," said Bollard, "we couldn't figure why the hell Thommassen went bad. I will be fucked. Jesus. The FBI just posted up a *Most Wanted* on him. They were staying out of this, right?"

"Yah," said Du Pré. He opened the shoehorn telephone and he punched the numbers into it.

A secretary answered.

"Wallace, it is Du Pré," said Du Pré.

"He'll be five minutes or so, Mister Du Pré. What is your number?" she said.

Du Pré recited the digits.

"What is going on?" said Bart.

"You maybe watch the road," said Du Pré. Bart's tires hit the rumble strip. He steered back to the flat pavement.

Du Pré rolled a smoke and he lit it and opened the window a crack.

He finished and flipped the butt out the window. The phone beeped.

"Doooo Preyyyyy," said Harvey Wallace.

"You are in this now?" said Du Pré.

"Oh, yes," said Harvey. "You know, Torbert Thommassen, the spook, turned out to be a spook for rent. Seems that there's a fellow over the river there who long suspected old Torbert of being for sale, but they couldn't get any proof. Then, of a sudden, some proof appeared. What proof they will not tell us, or how they came to get it, but judging from the uproar I'd say old Torbert sold some really good stuff to the Russians or the Chinese or somebody our government, such as it is, really resents. They are going batshit, actually. They wish to find Torbert in the worst way."

"OK," said Du Pré.

"Never made sense did it," said Harvey. "Long and honorable service, makes over a hundred grand a year as Milbank's security director, and of a sudden he goes in for kidnapping and all. Needed enough money to bribe a small country into letting him hide there. It's expensive."

"The money, the forty million, was sent," said Du Pré.

"So I hear," said Harvey. "You understand money these days? I never did. My wife says I am a financial imbecile. She gives me an allowance."

"So what now?" said Du Pré.

"Oh," said Harvey, "well, agents are converging on little old Billings from Denver and Salt Lake City. The Butte office is all on the way. Then I would expect all of those retired thugs who love to fly-fish and so they now live in Montana have been called up. Should be a lot of dust. I doubt it will mean a lot. Torbert was really cutting it close there. They are also very upset about that. They just found out and presumed they could close in on him. But somehow he knew, which in their world means there are *sinners*. The ungodly live in the house of spooks. I think they spend so much time playing Dungeons and Dragons for keeps they are all barking mad."

"Shit," said Du Pré.

"I wouldn't worry about Torbert," said Harvey. "He's only interested in getting away. He won't do anything to Julie or the Burrows. It is anyone around him you got to worry about. They could panic."

"Yah," said Du Pré.

"So," said Harvey, "why are you going to Billings?"

"They are there, probably," said Du Pré.

"Gabriel," said Harvey, "remember this. Torbert did this for a long time. He will have thought about all of this. He will know that you will think those people are in Billings. They very well may be. They very well could not be, too. So don't get too fixed on their being there. Torbert is smart, very smart, and he has the best training there is. Kidnapping is a crime usually committed by idiots. If Torbert thought this was his best chance, he was very careful. He isn't dumb and he isn't crazy and he is really dangerous if you get in his way. If anyone gets killed in this, it will be the people he recruited. Those fools Soldner and Henkel. They got into trouble, big trouble, they were embezzling and violating just about every rule there is on money except printing it yourself. Torbert must have found out and lured them in. He put this all together in a month. The spooks wanted to keep it quiet, of course, so they screwed around figuring out how to cover their asses. I love Washington. It's like a big high school where the popular kids have nukes and navies and other toys."

Du Pré laughed.

"Torbert won't do anything unnecessary," said Harvey. "Those other crapheads, who knows. I sincerely hope Torbert done liquidated them, myself. It's harsh, but there I am."

Du Pré shut up the telephone.

"What?" said Bart.

Du Pré told him.

"Jesus *Christ*," said Bart.

"I think," said Bollard, "that we had better handle this, Mister Fascelli. No offense, but that is what we get paid for. We know how to do this."

Bart looked at Du Pré.

"What do you think?" he said.

Du Pré shook his head.

"I don't know, this," he said. "There will be people all over Billings now. Maybe there is not so much that we can do."

"Go back?" said Bart.

Du Pré looked out the window.

Birds. Earth. Jackrabbit. Life.

Bart slowed and stopped on a snowplow turnaround.

Two other SUVs pulled in behind him.

"Thanks," said Bollard, "we get paid to guard you, Mister Fascelli. I'll go in one of the wagons. The other will follow you back."

Bart gripped the steering wheel.

"It's my fault," he said.

Du Pré sighed. He got out and walked round to the driver's door and he jerked it open and Bart got out and moved to the passenger seat. Bollard climbed in the first of the SUVs that had been following them.

"It is not your fault wanting to live your life," said Du Pré. "It is maybe the fault of that asshole Milbank who started this, here."

"It's the fucking money," said Bart. "I ought to get it in cash and burn it."

Du Pré snorted.

He turned the SUV back on to the highway and got up to speed.

"This was too easy," said Bart.

He looked at Du Pré.

Du Pré nodded.

"What?" said Bart.

Du Pré shook his head.

"I am wrong some, maybe I am wrong a lot," said Du Pré.

Bart got a can of pop out of the cooler. He offered it to Du Pré.

Du Pré shook his head.

"What are you going to do?" he said.

"Go to Toussaint," said Du Pré, "have a cheeseburger, fries, drink, maybe two. Talk to Madelaine."

Bart opened the can with a hissy pop.

"There is something else, isn't there?" he said.

Du Pré shrugged.

"Is Julie going to be all right?" he said.

Du Pré shrugged.

"Like Harvey said," said Du Pré, "it is not Thommassen who would kill her, the others, it is those fools of Milbank's, that Soldner and Henkel."

"Not much comfort," said Bart.

The SUV that had been following them slowed and stopped by the road.

"Should we check on them?" said Bart.

Du Pré shook his head.

"I wish," said Bart, "you would let me know what it is you are thinking."

"I don't know," said Du Pré. "When I know I tell you."

They went on in silence and they came to Toussaint and pulled up in front of the saloon.

They got out and went in.

Madelaine was beading the gauntlet she had been working on for three months. She nodded when they came in.

"Billings not so good?" she said.

Du Pré laughed.

"Milbank wants to buy this place," said Madelaine. "Susan Klein told him to go fuck himself."

"Two hours until we know where they are," said Bart.

Du Pré nodded, and Madelaine gave him a ditch.

CHAPTER

37

Julie and Conor and Eamon Burrows were walking around in the forest when Du Pré and Bart and the security detail got there. They were scratching and laughing.

Julie ran to Bart and she hugged him.

Du Pré went to Eamon and Conor.

"The last six hours were the worst," he said. "Looking at that damned digital display. And not knowing whether the motor home would blow up if we opened the door. Or a window and tried to crawl out. That guy seemed to have thought of everything."

"You were here all along?" said Du Pré.

"Didn't move an inch," said Eamon Burrows.

They were far back on an old logging road, well buried in a thick stand of firs. It was difficult to see where the road went off another that was almost as bad. When the directions came in, Du Pré had had to think hard. It was in a new-growth forest that had been planted in the 1930s.

There was a camouflage tarp over the top of the motor home so that it could not be easily seen from the air.

"You are OK?" said Du Pré.

"I stink," said Eamon. "I need a bath. No, there was food, even some booze, and the chemical toilet. Water, so we could wash a little. The first day, we were kept handcuffed. After carefully repeating several times how the thing was booby-trapped and escape was impossible, he let us loose. I know a little about wiring. I thought he probably meant business."

"Clear," said one of the security men, crawling out from under the motor home with a package wrapped in duct tape.

Eamon walked to him and the others followed.

"Was there a bomb?" he said.

The security man nodded.

"Woulda been nothing left but a hole in the ground," he said. "I expect this is C-4 or perhaps something even worse. Really simple, the way it was set up, but there was no way to get at anything from inside. Good thing you didn't try to get out. He meant it."

"I thought he did," said Burrows.

"Torbert Thommassen," said the security man, "and here I thought he was one of the good guys. My dad worked with him."

Conor and Julie were holding each other.

"Come on," said Bart. "I'll take you to my place."

Eamon Burrows pointed at another tarp. He pulled it off and there was his old battered Volvo.

"I'll follow," he said. He looked in the car.

He got in and started it and it purred.

Bart and Julie and Conor went to Bart's big green SUV and they got in and drove off.

Du Pré sighed and he walked slowly back to his cruiser.

He got in and he sat for a moment.

A white Cadillac bucked and jumped down the road and it lurched over a hump and Du Pré winced as he heard metal screech.

The Cadillac stopped.

Markham Milbank got out.

He looked at the motor home for a while and then he saw Du Pré and he waved listlessly.

"Took us all off," he said, "but thank God Julie and Conor and Eamon are OK. That was the main thing."

Du Pré looked at him.

He started his cruiser and he drove out to the branch road and then down to the country road to Toussaint and the saloon.

There were several government sedans parked in front, and two had suited men in them.

Du Pré sighed and he went in.

There were several agents eating hamburgers and talking in low tones at the big table by the window.

Susan Klein was at the bar. She made Du Pré a ditch and she pushed it over and he picked it up and he drank it.

Allison Ames was in a corner, staring off into space. She had a brandy glass in front of her with a stiff shot in it.

"Six of 'em," said Susan. "She came for the last one I told her she couldn't have it unless she rented a room out back. So she did."

Du Pré nodded.

He went over to her and he looked down.

"I . . . am . . . such . . . a . . . fool," she said. She went back to staring at the table.

The agents looked up when the door opened and Benny Klein came in. He looked at them warily.

"I'll take you there now," he said, "but I am goin' right now."

The agents looked at each other and they got up and left money on the table and they all went out.

"Poor Benny," said Susan, "poor baby. They are such rude bastards."

"Where is that Madelaine?" said Du Pré.

"Went out to Bart's, I guess," said Susan.

Du Pré had another drink and he went back to the cooler and he opened the door.

The banana crate was gone.

He shook his head.

He went out the back door and to Allison Ames's little white SUV and he looked in.

It wasn't there.

Du Pré looked over at the huge motor home that Markham Milbank used for an office.

He shook his head and he got in his cruiser and he drove out to Bart's.

Everyone was in the kitchen. Bart was washing dishes. Julie and Conor and Eamon looked wet and clean.

"Du Pré," said Madelaine, "you are here. I want to know why there are not ten FBIs here asking questions."

Du Pré shrugged.

Bart turned around.

"They want Torbert Thommassen," he said, "very badly. They'll be by just as soon as they get him."

Du Pré laughed.

Madelaine looked at him and shrugged.

Du Pré got some coffee and he sat down next to Eamon.

"You are coming to the roadhouse," he said, "what happens?"

"We stopped at a stop sign and out he came," said Eamon. "Handcuffed us, slapped a tow bar on the Volvo, and drove us to the motor home. Stuck us in it and patiently explained we would be blown to hell if we tried to leave. Then he left and came back and left and came back. We had television and food and everything but a shower. He said the tank was too small, and we needed to conserve water. He was always polite. Never once turned his back or gave any opportunity to jump him. He would have shrugged me off like a bug anyway, I'm sure."

Du Pré nodded.

"Forty million," said Eamon. "That should keep him well fixed wherever he goes."

"Ain't what it used to be," said Bart. "Never was in the first place."

"Jesus," said Julie, "I hated being cooped up in that place. I want to go and fly my ultralight."

"Young lady," said Bart, "have a heart. Pity your poor old uncle. Tomorrow. I have had enough worry."

The door opened and old Booger Tom came in, shaking his hand.

"Whooeee," he said, "slammed it in the danged gate."

Madelaine looked at it. She got a paper clip and she heated it with Du Pré's cigarette lighter and she punched a hole in the fingernail to let out the blood.

"I'm riding a little," said Booger Tom.

"Me, too," said Julie, "since I can't fly."

"That goddamned thing," said Booger Tom.

She went off and got her boots and she came back soon enough and the two of them went out.

Conor had been silent. Eamon put his hand on his son's shoulder.

"What is all this?" said Madelaine.

Bart brought coffee and he sat down.

"Old stuff coming to light," he said. "Thommassen had been playing dirty when he was a spy, and it was coming out, and he needed the money, I guess. He'll need a lot of it if they are as mad at him as they seem to be."

"James Bond shit?" said Madelaine.

Bart nodded.

"Do you understand it?" he said to Du Pré.

Du Pré shook his head.

"Not my world," he said.

"Any of us," said Bart.

"It turned out all right," said Eamon Burrows.

Du Pré nodded. He put some bourbon in his coffee. It smelled wonderful. He breathed deep.

"Du Pré," whispered Madelaine, "you are not saying everything you are thinking."

"Stay out of trouble that way," said Du Pré.

"Is this over?" said Madelaine.

"*Non,*" said Du Pré.

She looked at him for a long time and then she patted his hand.

"Some coyotes they get away," she said.

Du Pré nodded.

"Usually," he said, "they get away."

Madelaine laughed.

The telephone rang and Bart answered it.

He looked over at Du Pré.

"For you," he said, and he put the phone down on the counter.

CHAPTER

38

Du Pré wound up the drive that led to Benetsee's cabin. It was dark and there was no smoke coming out of the pipe, no sign that the old man had been there.

There was a nondescript Buick about twenty years old parked next to the porch.

Du Pré pulled along beside it and he got out.

"Afternoon," said Torbert Thommassen. He came up from the ground somehow.

Du Pré held his hands out by his sides.

Thommassen went to the Buick and he opened the trunk and he took out the banana crate with the Lewis and Clark artifacts in it and he set it on Du Pré's trunk lid.

"Didn't think you'd believe me otherwise," he said.

Du Pré nodded.

"So," he said, "why you do this?"

Thommassen took a flask out of his jacket and he had a swig and he offered it to Du Pré.

Du Pré shook his head.

"I got set up," he said, "by that good friend of mine Paul Beck. Twice, as it turns out. It is why I killed him. You know, he was smart and I trusted him and I did that in a business you cannot trust anyone in."

Du Pré nodded.

"They will get you I think," he said.

"Probably," said Thommassen. "They've gotten a little better than they were before the Arabs bombed us with our own planes. Not that much better. No, I probably can't make it. I hope you told someone where you were going."

Du Pré nodded.

"Your woman," said Thommassen, "lovely woman. Well. I had this set up, and damned if those little turds Henkel and Soldner didn't come to me with a bullshit proposition that they thought sounded good. Little assholes, they oughta rot in a nice prison for about the rest of their lives."

Du Pré sat down on the edge of the porch and he rolled a smoke and lit it and he watched the blue stream rise up from the tip.

"So," said Thommassen, "do you want to know what actually happened?"

Du Pré nodded.

"Henkel and Soldner were going to kidnap Markham Milbank, and they knew I was unhappy guarding the little shit, so they made a proposition, which I declined. They came back again, and I said, well, there is a way this could work. In the interim, word had come to me that an old Russian attempt to frame me had been dug up and taken for the truth. You make enemies in this business, and because we deal in mortal stuff, mortal enemies. So I told them that it would be easier to get Milbank to pay for the Lewis and Clark material. So that is where it started, and indeed I planned to rip them off and be gone. But they couldn't leave well enough alone, and they kept adding idiocy to foolishness, and so soon it was an attack on Julie Perelli and that hilarious scoundrel of a bass player . . ."

"Those two guys burned up down in Billings?" said Du Pré.

"Henkel and Soldner hired them, of course. They were just cons. Dumb as dirt and dangerous. They were the ones who actually attacked Julie and Bassman, and they were going to ambush the Burrows and Julie. So I got there first. No harm done, unless you count kidnapping and murder, even if they needed it. Don't you say out here that someone needed killing?"

Du Pré nodded.

"So," he said, "what you do now?"

"Try to catch up to the money," said Thommassen. "I figure I have an even chance if I don't make any mistakes."

"Soldner, Henkel?" said Du Pré.

"Never thought you'd ask," said Thommassen. "They are well doped up and sleeping in the shed by the old Great Northern railroad tracks where they cross the creek just east of the crossroads."

Du Pré laughed.

"There's a video disc there, too, upon which they confess to all. So, Mister Du Pré, what do we do now?"

Du Pré looked at him.

"Go," he said, "maybe you are lying to me but I do not think so. You break a bunch of laws but you got reasons. Maybe you make it. Maybe you don't. I don't help them till it is dark, and then I don't help them much. We let God decide this, eh?"

Thommassen stood up, and he offered Du Pré his hand.

Du Pré took it.

"Good luck," said Thommassen, "I think you are one of those people who always finds trouble without meaning to."

Du Pré laughed.

Thommassen went to his car and he got in and turned round and drove out and he turned right and he was gone.

Du Pré walked back to the little creek where the sweat lodge was and he sat on the cut stump and he watched the birds.

A kingfisher clattered past, a flash of blue and white, and it was gone.

Du Pré had some whiskey and a couple of cigarettes and then he went to his old cruiser and he got in and he drove down to the east-west highway and he headed toward the crossroads forty miles away.

He whistled as he drove.

"Maybe, maybe not," he said to the air, "but if not, there is no reason for Thommassen not to kill me or try to."

The shed stood beside the old tracks, still in use but in poor repair, and Du Pré drove over the cattle guard and he parked by the racked yellow building. The door was open. The air was a fug, sweet and nasty.

Two men lay on sleeping bags in the dirt. One moaned a little.

Du Pré went back to the cruiser and he turned the radio on. The dispatcher who hated him finally answered.

"It is Du Pré," said Du Pré. "Tell him I have two bodies, the old shed out by the tracks the crossroads."

"That's a message?" said the dispatcher. "What shed? Where are you exactly?"

Du Pré repeated what he had said.

"What the fuck kind of directions are those?" said the dispatcher.

A voice sounded behind her.

"What?" said Benny, over the radio.

"Out the crossroads," said Du Pré, "I got two guys here, you arrest them you come. They are drugged."

"What two guys?" said Benny.

"Those guys with Milbank kidnapped Julie, the Burrows," said Du Pré.

"Jesus," said Benny, "I'll be right there."

He shut the radio off.

Du Pré smoked.

He had some more whiskey.

He looked in on Henkel and Soldner.

Both of them were stirring a little and moaning.

Du Pré went in and he found the disc in its plastic case sitting on one of the old boxes stacked in a corner.

He put it in his pocket.

He went back outside and he had another cigarette.

"Bullshit," said Du Pré. "It is all bullshit."

He yawned.

A helicopter appeared on the eastern horizon and it was making straight for Du Pré.

"Eavesdroppers," said Du Pré. He sighed and he went back into the shed and he put the disc back where it had been.

Henkel's eyes were half open.

Neither he nor Soldner was tied up at all.

"That Thommassen, he knew what I would do," said Du Pré.

The helicopter was getting closer.

Du Pré sat on the hood of his old cruiser, sipping whiskey and smoking.

The helicopter came close and circled him. A man in a dark suit was looking out the open window and jabbering into a mouthpiece. The helicopter did not land, it just circled.

A line of three tan government sedans shot over the top of the hill to the east, and they began to slow down and then they turned on to the rutted road that led to the old shed.

Two of the cars blocked Du Pré in. The FBI agents got out, guns drawn.

Du Pré yawned.

His cell phone chirred in the car. He looked at it for a moment. It chirred again. Du Pré picked it up.

"Good afternoon," said Harvey Wallace. "Where is that prick Thommassen?"

"I don't see him," said Du Pré.

"How did you find whoever you found then?" said Harvey.

"Birds," said Du Pré. "They talk, I listen."

Harvey was silent for a moment.

"Is it Henkel and Soldner?" he said.

"Yah," said Du Pré.

"That son of a bitch," said Harvey. "Damn, he is good."

"These guys, yours," said Du Pré, "got their guns out."

"Pointed at you?" said Harvey.

"Non," said Du Pré, "they are just glaring."

"Give the phone to one of them," said Harvey.

Du Pré handed it to the agent nearest him.

Benny Klein's cruiser turned in.

Du Pré nodded.

The agent with the cell phone was looking at Du Pré and saying *yeah* into it.

Du Pré got in his cruiser and he drove off through the grass and back out to the highway.

Benny Klein stopped and he rolled down his window.

"Assholes," he said.

Du Pré yawned.

"Let them have them," he said. "You don't really want them now, do you?"

Benny looked at Du Pré.

Then they both laughed.

CHAPTER

39

Du Pré and Benetsee stood up when Judge Clemens entered the room.

The judge sat and he looked out at the attorneys and Du Pré and Benetsee and a good three dozen reporters and the public three deep at the back of the room.

"Ralph," said Judge Clemens to the government attorney, "I really can't do much but dismiss all of this. The lot."

The government attorney glared at Du Pré and Benetsee.

"The stuff was fake and these guys know where the real Lewis and Clark artifacts and the journal are," said Ralph.

Judge Clemens nodded.

"You haven't established that any artifacts or journals were in fact indisputably connected to the Lewis and Clark Expedition," said Judge Clemens. "So far as we know, the fakes were fakes all along."

The government attorney grew red.

"All charges dismissed," said Judge Clemens. He rapped once with his gavel and he shot through the drapes that covered the door to his chambers.

Du Pré and Benetsee moved slowly through the mass of reporters. They did not say anything. When one particularly aggressive newsman planted himself in front of Benetsee the old man slowly looked up at him, and when their eyes met the reporter backed away.

One of Bart's big SUVs, dark green with heavily tinted windows, stood at the curb. Du Pré and Benetsee got into it.

"Around back?" said Bart.

"Yeah," said Du Pré, "there is this door says IN on it."

Bart pulled away, and he went round behind the building and down to the parking garage in the underground.

Judge Clemens was standing near the elevator, dressed in worn denims and cowboy boots and a stained and battered old hat. Bart pulled up and the judge got in and Bart went out into the sun.

The judge turned and he looked at Benetsee.

"The bones are being shipped," he said. "I will see that they get to you."

Benetsee grinned, showing some stubs of black teeth.

"They here now," he said.

Bart slowed down.

"Up there?" he said, pointing to the airport on the sandstone benches that rose above Billings. A big jet was swooping in.

Bart changed lanes and he turned right and they soon were at the terminal.

"Over there," said Judge Clemens, pointing to the freight terminal. Bart drove past a guard who did not even look up.

Judge Clemens got out and he went into the terminal office and he came back out a few minutes later. He filled his pipe and he lit it and he leaned against the SUV. Du Pré got out, too, and he rolled a smoke.

"You understand all of what went on?" said the judge.

Du Pré shook his head.

"Too rich here," he said. "America got too much money."

The judge nodded.

"The people who were kidnapped are all right?" said Judge Clemens.

Du Pré snorted.

"Yah," he said.

"I am curious," said the judge, "about the Lewis and Clark material. I suspect that the real things exist. I expect that the old man knows where they are."

Du Pré nodded.

"Strange," said the judge, "a few things lost and a couple of centuries later they get people killed."

"Fools," said Du Pré.

"Have you ever known any other medicine people like Benetsee?" said the judge.

"One, him, enough," said Du Pré. "Old joker, Old Coyote. Him like drive people crazy."

"I don't agree," said the judge. "I think that Benetsee tries to teach people to see what is really there."

"Yah," said Du Pré, "people, they can't handle what is really there, most."

"How old do you think he is?" said the judge.

"Him old," said Du Pré, "when my grandfather he knows him. He is old then."

A clerk appeared at an open door. He held a box about the size of the banana box that Du Pré had hidden the fake Lewis and Clark stuff in.

"Ah," said the judge, "time for my signature."

He tapped out his pipe and he went in and he soon came back with the box, a waxed carton with plastic seals and bands.

Bart popped the rear door open and the judge put the box in the back and he closed the door and then he and Du Pré got in.

"Drop me back at the Federal Building," said Judge Clemens. "I wonder if it would be all right if I came to the funeral for those people back there."

Benetsee looked at him.

"Honor the dead," said Benetsee. "You help them come home they would like you there."

"When will that be?" said the judge.

"Soon as we get back," said Benetsee. "They been out of their earth a long time gone. Very tired of that."

"I can have you flown back here," said Bart.

"Good," said Judge Clemens. "That would be very good."

Bart headed east on the Interstate and then he turned north and he drove on the two-lane blacktop.

He kept the speed legal.

"Does this goddamned thing go any faster?" said Judge Clemens. "I'm from North Dakota, you see."

Du Pré laughed. He fished a flask out of his jacket and he had some whiskey and he rolled down the window and he made up two cigarettes. He lit them both and he passed the first to Benetsee. The old man sighed and puffed.

They did not speak again until they got to Toussaint.

Madelaine was behind the bar, beading another purse. She didn't look up when they came in.

"Du Pré!" she said, "that judge don't throw you in the can forever!"

"*Non,*" said Du Pré.

"*Non,*" said Judge Clemens.

Father Van Den Heuvel came out of the men's room. He tripped over a chair leg and he fell halfway and he caught himself and he came on.

"OK," said Madelaine. She put the purse down. She put her reading glasses on top of it.

Judge Clemens smiled at her.

"I'm the judge who didn't throw Du Pré in jail," he said.

"Why not, you son of a bitch," said Madelaine and they both laughed.

Madelaine put the sign on the bartop.

MIX AND PAY YOUR OWN DAMN SELF. RIGHT BACK.

They went out to the SUV and Du Pré got the box with the Métis bones in it and they walked up the street to the little cemetery behind the white clapboard Catholic Church. There was a blanket spread on the ground beside a newly dug grave.

Du Pré cut the seals and he opened the box and he carefully lifted out the bones and skulls and he put them in the red blanket and then he folded it round them and he stepped down in the grave and he put the bundle gently down and he got out again.

Father Van Den Heuvel said the burial service and Benetsee began to sing, his old voice high and clear.

It did not take very long.

Bart and Du Pré filled the grave while Benetsee made tobacco around it.

Benetsee was still in his finery.

They walked back toward the saloon, but when they passed the little creek that ran through town Benetsee turned off and he began to trot up the path that ran beside it. For all his years he moved very swiftly.

"That," said the judge, "is undoubtedly the greatest man in Montana."

"You could maybe hang him for that?" said Du Pré.

Everyone laughed.

Four ranchers were sitting at the bar with the drinks they had made.

"Shit," said one, "now we gotta pay fer 'em."

Madelaine went back to her stool behind the bar and she smiled at the four while Du Pré and Bart and the judge and the priest took stools down at the far end.

The till was open and four dollars lay on the ledge above the drawer for tips.

"Shake?" said Madelaine. She got the dice cup and they began to play for the pot, a jerky container that held a gallon of mixed small bills.

"I miss this," said the judge. "There was a place just like this in the little town I grew up in. Everybody went there. This feels like that place."

"A good place," said Bart.

The telephone rang and Du Pré went to answer it so Madelaine could go on shaking dice with the ranchers.

"Yah," he said.

"We got him," said Harvey. "Of course he stuck his pistol in his mouth when he saw the cars. So that's over."

"Harvey," said Du Pré, "any of this make any sense, you?"

"None whatever," said Harvey. "I have to admit a good deal of what people do makes no sense at all. For instance, we have nuclear weapons—."

"Why him do this?" said Du Pré.

"Why anyone?" said Harvey. "He damn near made it, though. Had a plane there and he was about thirty seconds from being airborne and gone in the night. We could maybe have tracked him but then again maybe not. Well, he can't explain it now anyway."

"Lewis and Clark stuff, it was fake," said Du Pré.

"I'm sure it was," said Harvey. "And where is Benetsee?"

"Holding up the world," said Du Pré.

"You know," said Harvey, "finding things is all right, but the looking for them is a lot better."

They both laughed.

Du Pré hung up the telephone.

"Bassman call," said Madelaine. "They want you play that roadhouse, next Friday."

"Where is it?" said Judge Clemens.

"Down on the Missouri," said Madelaine, "new people, but they are very nice."

"Maybe that Kim kill him this time," said Du Pré.

CHAPTER

40

The wind blew with force.

The door of the Toussaint Saloon banged open and banged shut and banged open again.

"Christ," said Booger Tom, " 'bout enough to blow the hair off a dog."

Bart came back to his stool and he stood there.

Du Pré got up.

"You watch that wind, Du Pré," said Madelaine, "you are flying when you go over hills sometimes."

Du Pré laughed.

Bart went out and Du Pré after him and they got into Du Pré's old cruiser and a tumbleweed got stuck in the windshield wiper for a moment and then it tore away.

"I'd drive," said Bart. "I suppose I could."

His left hand was in a nylon cast. He had broken some of the bones in it when a torque wrench sheared off a bolt.

"*Non,*" said Du Pré.

He got to the north-south highway and he turned left and he

gunned the big engine. The cruiser got up to ninety-five quick enough.

"I got a call from Markham Milbank," said Bart. "He wondered what he could do to help anyone that all this hurt."

Du Pré snorted.

"It is too much money," he said.

"That's what I said," said Bart. "I told him he was a fat hog and everyone wants a slice."

Du Pré nodded.

"They don't have schools," said Bart, "to teach you how to be rich."

The wind rose and screamed and dust devils raced across the High Plains, and rows of tumbleweeds danced over the road.

The heavy old cruiser rocked on its springs whenever the wind gusted. But it sat down on the road low enough so there wasn't much for the wind to grasp.

"One of my Suburbans would be in the ditch," said Bart.

Du Pré nodded. He rolled himself a smoke and he lit it and he sucked in a good lungful.

"Where does Benetsee have the real stuff from the expedition?" said Bart.

Du Pré shook his head.

"That old goat," said Bart, "is ahead of us all."

Du Pré nodded.

A huge motor home appeared on the top of the next hill, pushed a good thirty degrees off plumb.

Du Pré braked and he slowed and he turned off on a county road.

The motor home sailed past.

"Smart," said Bart.

"There it goes," said Du Pré.

The motor home had tipped over and it was coming apart.

"Shit," said Du Pré.

"Shit," said Bart.

Du Pré turned and he drove back to the mess of aluminum sheeting and household goods strewn over the highway and the downwind verge.

A man was struggling out of the wreckage.

Du Pré and Bart got out of the cruiser.

The man looked at them.

"You all right?" said Bart.

"Not at all," said the man. "I'll need you to drive me to the nearest place I can get some help for this."

"Anyone else in this thing?" said Bart.

"Just me," said the man.

"Good," said Bart. "Fuck you, and you can wait until someone comes along who gives a shit, and that ain't us."

Du Pré and Bart got back in the cruiser. Du Pré backed and turned.

"I'll sue you sons of bitches," screamed the man.

"Don't worry," said Bart. "Somebody will kill him."

Du Pré laughed and he punched the accelerator and they were soon back to the usual ninety-five.

There was little traffic. Anyone with a grain of sense was home.

They got to the Interstate and Du Pré turned west and he slowed down to seventy-five.

Semis going past on the opposite lanes were laboring against the wind. The few ahead of the cruiser in the westbound lanes were weaving from the wind shoving the trailers against the tractors.

"I don't recall it blowing this hard," said Bart.

"It does," said Du Pré, "from the east there is a bad storm coming maybe."

"Freaky weather this year," said Bart.

"Montana we got no other kind," said Du Pré.

They got to Billings and Du Pré drove on up to the airport and he stopped in front of the passenger terminal.

"Thanks," said Bart. "Go on home to that lovely woman." He took his briefcase and small suitcase out of the trunk and he slammed the lid.

Du Pré waved as he drove away.

Twenty miles east of Billings Du Pré slowed and stopped. There had been an accident and a semitrailer was slaunchwise across the eastbound lanes. Loose sheets of aluminum flapped in the wind on the wrecked trailer. The tractor was on its side.

Two giant tow trucks were cabling the mess out of the way.

A highway patrolman walked back to Du Pré's cruiser.

He bent down.

"A few minutes," he said.

"OK," said Du Pré.

The highway patrolman was young and he looked very lost so someone had died.

The two tow trucks winched the wreckage away and Du Pré was waved on through and he waited until he was a mile away before speeding up.

He got to the north-south highway that led home and he turned off and crossed over the Interstate and he gunned the engine and got up to ninety-five. Like God intended for folks to drive at in Montana, which was very big and pretty empty.

Du Pré rolled a smoke and he lit it and when he had stubbed out the butt he reached under the seat for his flask and he fished it out and shook it. There was only a teaspoon or so in it.

"God damn . . . forgot to fill it, stupid bastard," he said pleasantly.

He shoved the flask back under the seat.

A few miles ahead there was a roadhouse off on the right, in the middle of nowhere.

Du Pré pulled in to the lot and he parked and he went in.

A pleasant-looking woman looked up.

"Afternoon," she said.

A man in a wheelchair grinned at Du Pré. He had coppery skin and a round face. Mexican, probably, Du Pré thought.

Most of them Indians, too.

"I have a ditch," said Du Pré, "fifth of that Jim Beam maybe too."

The woman mixed his drink and set it over and then she went to the cabinet where the brown goods were stored and she got out a fifth of whiskey and she put it in a paper sack.

She put two dollars on the bar.

"Every year they stick on more taxes," she said.

"See you," said the man in the wheelchair. He rolled it toward the door and he pulled the door open and he struggled through it and the door shut hard.

"Poor Luis," said the woman. "Got the crap kicked out of him a few weeks ago and they hurt him pretty bad."

"Fight?" said Du Pré. The man had looked far too pleasant to fight.

"No," she said. "We had a country band here, and a lot of folks had come and Luis just went out to his van to get some smokes, I think. Anyway he got jumped and the hell beat out of him. Luis is a nice guy and it made no sense at all."

Du Pré sipped his drink.

"All the years we have had this place," said the woman, "that was the first time anything like that happened. Oh, you know, fellers get a few in 'em and then they go on out in the lot there and punch the spots off each other but this was just senseless. Luis has a little place, been here all his life, and he is about the sweetest person. Probably some bastards from Billings."

Du Pré nodded.

Another couple came in the door and the woman went down the bar to talk with them.

She said something and they all laughed.

They played dice for the pot, but the couple lost.

Du Pré rolled a smoke.

He finished his drink.

He lit his cigarette.

The woman behind the bar spotted his empty glass and she bustled back down to fix him another.

Du Pré fished out another five-dollar bill.

"The night Luis is beaten up," he said, "anything else happen?"

The woman nodded.

"The Mosely girl went out just ahead of Luis to get something out of her car and somebody sprayed her in the face with that mace stuff."

Du Pré nodded.

"Maybe the same guys beat up Luis," said the woman, "but they didn't do anything more."

"Put that in a go-cup," said Du Pré.

The woman dumped the ditch in a plastic cup and Du Pré waved at the change.

There was an old poster tacked to the wall outside.

Du Pré looked at the date.

"Son of a bitch," he said.

CHAPTER

41

"Du Pré, you are thinking so loud you are cracking the paint," said Madelaine. She drew her fingers across his chest.

Du Pré sighed.

"Wind blow your voice away?" she said.

"Better I don't talk this," said Du Pré. "Maybe later I talk."

"That bad?" said Madelaine.

"Yah," said Du Pré.

He got up and he pulled on his clothes and boots. It was afternoon yet, but suppertime wasn't far off.

"I hold some dinner for you," said Madelaine.

"*Non,*" said Du Pré. "I get a burger maybe later."

"It is not over," said Madelaine.

Du Pré shook his head. He got his hat from the rack as he went past and he went out to his cruiser. He got in and he drove out to Bart's and he parked by the house.

Julie was up in the air. The wind had died away and the air was clear.

Conor and Eamon Burrows were sitting in folding chairs drinking sodas.

Du Pré sat on the steps of the deck and he sighed and he rolled a cigarette. Booger Tom came round one of the outbuildings and he saw Du Pré and he walked over, one leg stiff.

"Danged roan horse tossed me," said Booger Tom. "I ain't as young as I was and haven't been for some time."

He grabbed the rail and he lowered himself down.

"Missy is having the time of her life," said Booger Tom.

Du Pré nodded.

The old cowboy looked at Du Pré for a long time.

"Yer belt a notch too tight or you thinkin' good finally," said Booger Tom.

Du Pré sighed and he shook his head.

"I tol' you you was wrong there," said Booger Tom.

"Yah," said Du Pré, "but you were not right, either."

Booger Tom looked up at Julie in her little ultralight.

"Shit," he said. "She will have her heart broke."

"Maybe not," said Du Pré. "Not the boy. I see him that night he stays, but Eamon goes out."

"She won't never believe it," said Booger Tom. "Believe he didn't have anything to do with it."

"*Non,*" said Du Pré.

"Life is shitty sometimes," said Booger Tom.

Du Pré nodded and he got up and he stretched.

Eamon Burrows said something to Conor and they laughed and then Eamon began to walk back toward the house.

Du Pré went up to the fence and he waited.

Eamon Burrows looked right at Du Pré as he came and his face was set.

He stopped two feet away.

They said nothing for a time.

"Thomassen said you would dig it all out in time," said Eamon Burrows.

Du Pré nodded.

"Conor had nothing to do with it," said Burrows. "Not any idea. I was losing the boatyard."

Du Pré nodded.

Burrows turned and he looked up at Julie banking over the barns.

He held out his hand.

"I'll take care of it," he said. "You have my word. I did something that can't be fixed."

Du Pré nodded.

"Gives them a chance maybe," he said.

"Everybody ought to get a chance," said Eamon Burrows. He walked over to his Volvo and he got in and he started it and he wheeled away and he went out toward the country road.

Du Pré walked on.

Conor was looking up at Julie, who was bringing the little plane lower and getting ready to land.

"I thought you were Dad," he said when he looked at Du Pré.

"*Non*," said Du Pré. "He said he had to go and get something."

Conor nodded and he looked away for a moment and then back at Du Pré and then at his father's car, now heading west on the county road.

He looked at Du Pré again and then he looked away.

Conor went back to looking at Julie, up in the air.

He scratched himself absently.

Du Pré looked at the country road. He stared for a moment.

He looked at the stand of Russian olives that grew in the seep by the road, a quarter mile down it.

"Got to take a leak," said Conor. He turned and walked swiftly toward the house.

Du Pré waited until the boy went in the door, and then he began to run hard across the pasture toward the stand of trees.

A strip of tall dark green sedges followed the buried little creek toward the Russian olives. Du Pré dropped down behind them, screened from the house. He went toward the road hunched over, sometimes on his hands and knees.

The little motor on Julie's ultralight snarled and then another joined in, and Conor shot out from the barn on a small motorcycle, racing down the long drive to the county road.

Du Pré looked over, saw the boy looking ahead, avoiding the ruts,

211

and he stood up then and ran again and came to the thick stand of pale dusty trees.

Eamon Burrows stood by the Volvo, a chopped shotgun in his hands. He had turned away a moment to look to the boy, now rounding the corner of the main gate.

Du Pré stepped out from the trees, his nine-millimeter in his hands, pointing the barrel at the ground ahead of him.

Eamon Burrows turned then and saw Du Pré and his face flushed red and he began to raise the shotgun and Du Pré swung up and pulled the trigger twice and Eamon Burrows was picked up by the slugs and slammed against the side of his Volvo.

He leaned against it for a moment, looking curiously at his chest, and then he dropped the shotgun.

The ultralight snarled overhead, and Conor on the little motorcycle was coming up the road, accelerating, hunched down over the bars, his face hidden.

Du Pré sighed. He walked to the front of the Volvo, so it was between him and the motorcycle and the boy.

The shotgun boomed then and Du Pré jumped, and then a tire hissed as it lost air.

Du Pré stood on the bumper.

The boy got nearer.

Then the cycle began to slow down and Conor dropped it on the road and he rushed to his father and he grabbed his shoulders and tried to lift him.

"No!" screamed Conor. "No!"

Du Pré stood near, his feet on the shotgun.

The boy put his head on his father's chest and he sobbed.

A pickup truck came out of the ranch drive, and soon Booger Tom was there, his old hogleg in his hand when he got out of the truck.

"This some shit?" said Booger Tom.

Conor Burrows sobbed, rocked his father in his arms.

He looked up at Du Pré.

"This is all your idea," said Du Pré. "Yes?"

Conor shook his head.

"Your father, him, losing his boatyard, you know this rich girl . . ." said Du Pré.

Conor looked away.

Du Pré bent down and he picked up the pump shotgun and he racked the shells out of it and left the breech open.

Du Pré tossed the shotgun shells off into the field.

Conor put his father down, he hugged himself. He moaned.

Julie in the ultralight flew over, high up, though.

"Freeze, you little bastard," said Booger Tom. He had the old Peacemaker up and aimed right at the boy's head. "Move one hair I will blow a hole in ya big enough fer an owl to nest in."

Du Pré came up to the boy, reached down, found the pistol he had in his hand, tugged it away.

Du Pré looked at the gun.

"Shit," he said.

All three of them looked at Julie, up in the air.